AMELIA ATWATER-RHODES

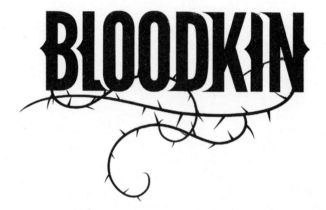

BLOODKIN

THE MAEVE'RA
VOLUME II

DELACORTE PRESS

Text copyright © 2015 by Amelia Atwater-Rhodes
Jacket art copyright © 2015 by Sammy Yuen

randomhouseteens.com

Educators and librarians, for a variety of teaching tools, visit us at RHTeachersLibrarians.com

Library of Congress Cataloging-in-Publication Data
Atwater-Rhodes, Amelia.
  Bloodkin / Amelia Atwater Rhodes. — First edition.
    pages cm. — (The Maeve'ra ; volume 2)
  Summary: When a shapeshifter/vampire nation is charged with a crime against Midnight that sixteen-year-old Kadee and her friend Vance played a hand in, Kadee feels compelled to return to the Shantel forest where she must confront her past and the decisions she has made in the pursuit of freedom.
  ISBN 978-0-385-74305-1 (hc) — ISBN 978-0-307-98075-5 (ebook)
  [1. Fantasy. 2. Shapeshifting—Fiction. 3. Vampires—Fiction.] I. Title.
  PZ7.A8925Bi 2015
  [Fic] —dc23
                                    2014020694

The text of this book is set in 12-point Loire.
Jacket design and interior design by Jinna Shin

Printed in the United States of America
10 9 8 7 6 5 4 3 2 1
First Edition

Bloodkin is dedicated to my father, William Rhodes.

Writing the Maeve'ra trilogy has involved some of the most intense historical research I have ever done. Balancing historical accuracy and detail with suspension of disbelief in a fantasy setting is always tough, and I'm never able to include all the fun tidbits of information I would love to share. Thankfully, my father is also a fan of history. Since I have been working on the Maeve'ra, we have had many fascinating conversations about everything from the role of women in the Revolutionary War to overseas trade in the beginning of the nineteenth century. I finally followed your advice, Dad—here's a story about the Revolutionary War for you. Kind of.

No acknowledgements page of mine would be complete without my giving thanks to my fellow writers and beta readers, who stuck with me as I went through draft after draft, adding and removing entire plotlines and multiple characters as I tried to get the story just right.

Finally, thanks to everyone at Random House, and to my wonderful editor, Jodi, for being so patient with me as I navigated life's ups and downs—and watched more than one deadline sail by in the meantime!

Welcome back to the Maeve'ra, everyone. Enjoy!

PROLOGUE

"WE HOLD THESE truths to be self-evident, that all men are created equal, that they are endowed by their Creator with certain unalienable Rights, that among these are Life, Liberty and the pursuit of Happiness. . . . That whenever any Form of Government becomes destructive of these ends, it is the Right of the People to alter or to abolish it. . . ."

My father taught me those words when I was just a child, too young to read them for myself. That was before I was taken away at age seven, and learned that I was something called serpiente, and that I had a people and a civilization.

And a king.

The serpiente claim to be the freest culture in the world, but that is an egotistical delusion. They worship freedom the way

1

corrupt men worship God: from afar, with faith that it must exist, but little loyalty and no personal experience. They bow to their king, who they call Diente, and even he bows to another, crueler power: Midnight, an empire ruled by blood-drinking immortals.

The vampires' empire maintains its grasp on those it rules through cruelty, slavery, and terror. The shapeshifter nations are too afraid to rise up, so they play Midnight's games. Kings exploit their own people in order to preserve their precious illusion of freedom.

My father taught me that an American does not accept an abusive government, that it is not just our right but our duty to stand up to a leader who mistreats us. Farrell, the man who took me in when I fled the serpiente palace three years ago, taught me a similar lesson: a child of Obsidian bows to no king, no queen. No Diente Julian. No Mistress of Midnight, the pale vampiress Jeshickah, who claims to rule the world. I accepted the name Obsidian proudly. It is true that we live as outlaws, but that is because the alternative is to live as slaves.

When I joined the Obsidian guild, they told me about a prophecy, which had been given years before by our kinsman Malachi when he and his mother had still been slaves in Midnight: someday, his then-unborn sister would take the serpiente throne and bring about the fall of the vampires' empire. Farrell rescued Malachi and his pregnant mother from Midnight and brought them back to the Obsidian guild to live freely.

I was told of the prophecy by Malachi and Misha's younger brother, Shkei, but the Obsidian guild doesn't actively concern itself with kings or queens, fate and the future. What will be, will be. A child of Obsidian is the master of his or her own life, not an arbiter of destiny.

We had hope for the days ahead, and that was enough—until last summer, when Misha, who was supposed to destroy Midnight, was instead sold to it as a slave. With her went Shkei, my dearest friend, a boy whose sixteen years of life were snuffed out to satisfy a bitter king.

I do not know how much one individual can accomplish alone, but I know what a group of people who have chosen complacency will accomplish together: nothing. I am not content to wash my hands of a world where these things happen, but sometimes it seems there are few other choices, and each one is worse than the last.

Kadee Obsidian
May 7, 1804

CHAPTER 1

PERFECT WEATHER FOR *a shopping trip,* I thought as I passed through the gates to the serpiente open-air market.

A fine, chilly drizzle was falling from the overcast May sky. Like everyone else in the market, I kept my head down so the hood of my cloak could keep the rain out of my eyes. Unlike everyone else, I had good reason to hide my face regardless of the weather: like most members of the Obsidian guild, I was wanted for treason. I did have the distinction of being guilty based on my own actions instead of just by association, which was the charge on most of Obsidian's members. I had been convicted at a trial I had declined to attend three years ago—wisely, since the sentence would have been death despite my age.

I was fifteen now, and grateful for the rain.

Under the cloak, I felt half naked in the clothes of a casual serpiente trader: a loose blouse under a half bodice, and trousers that hugged my hips and thighs, then laced even more tightly at my calves. The bodice was low-cut, and dyed a brilliant shade of emerald, leaving the majority of my chest exposed.

A good way to catch your death by lung fever, I thought, then shook my head. The concern was a remnant of another time, another life. Serpent shapeshifters like me were immune to human diseases like that.

Maybe that was why they were so comfortable wearing so little clothing.

Out of the corner of my eye, I spied the black and crimson uniform of a member of the palace guards. His gaze drifted over me as he scanned the crowd in the marketplace, but he paid me no attention. Why would he? I was just another shopper.

Unfortunately, "shopping" was made difficult by the fact that I had no trade goods or currency that I dared use. That meant I had to get creative.

Once, I would have balked at stealing, but these days, my hands were swift. As I moved casually through the marketplace, I took advantage of absentminded shopkeepers— those who were busy flirting, or whose eyes had caught on the brightly dressed dancers who flitted through the crowd. A salt horn, a bag of dried peas, a sack of cornmeal, and a log of goat cheese all disappeared into the haversack that hung at my hip.

I didn't take much from any individual merchant. I couldn't quite resist a warm lamb pie, which smelled of rich spices, but I slipped a blood coin onto the merchant's table where he would find it later.

Midnight called the currency it minted *trade* coins. However, since Midnight was just as quick to trade in slaves as in these pieces of metal, the more evocative name was far more popular. The vampires' empire protected the coins' value, so they were valid even here in the serpiente market, but there was no reason the local trader I was pretending to be would have them. I couldn't afford to draw attention to myself by using them openly, but I didn't like to outright steal something I didn't really *need*.

I was aware that this was a narrow distinction, but I made it anyway.

Food was a necessary resource, but that wasn't the only reason I risked coming to the serpiente market, which was open to the air and sky above but surrounded by high walls on all sides. The only way in or out was through the public areas of the palace, where being caught meant death, but ignorance was even more dangerous. While "shopping," I kept an ear out for gossip. Information was more valuable than gold.

This spring had resulted in a larger than normal number

of healthy lambs born, which was good news. Wool was one of the serpiente's key trade goods. Last year, a winter fever had ravaged the flocks, leaving the serpiente king unable to pay bills owed to masters with neither the patience nor the kindness to offer lenience.

The king had blamed the Obsidian guild. We were already guilty of treason, so why not add a charge of sheep poisoning? It gave him an excuse to send guards into the woods. It gave him an excuse to pay *his* bills with *our* flesh and blood: Shkei and Misha.

I had to stop there in the spitting rain and take a deep breath. Serpiente were very sensitive to the emotions of those around them, and nearby merchants and shoppers had started glancing at me with concern. I couldn't afford the attention. I was here because I was normally *better* than most of our guild at blending in and hiding any anxiety I might feel.

The memory, still raw less than a year later, had taken me by surprise. That was all.

I pretended to examine the trinkets at the nearest merchant's stall as I brought my emotions under control.

A group of dancers, two women and a man, came up beside me. Their bodies were wrapped in brilliantly colored scarves and little else, the cloth just enough to accentuate bare skin that had been painted with henna designs and in some places decorated with tiny rhinestones.

"I'm sorry," the merchant said. "I know I said I would

try to get more of those bone combs for you, but I haven't managed yet."

Bone combs? I wondered. I had seen a few dancers wearing fancy carved combs in their hair but hadn't given much thought to the silly things until now. The Shantel were famous for their bone and leather goods, but the Obsidian guild had a few talented carvers as well, and bone was a material easily acquired through hunting. If this was a popular item that had suddenly become rare, it might be a way to earn a few coins the next time we went to Midnight's market.

I chanced a glance up, and sure enough, one of the women was wearing one of the apparently coveted combs. It had been carved to resemble—what else?—a serpent, with an emerald-green body and a white diamond pattern down its back. The bone had been dyed and polished to such a shine that it glittered like a gem, brilliant against the dancer's dark hair.

As I watched, the snake moved, shifting its coils and blinking its eyes.

Magic, I thought with disappointment. There were people in my guild capable of making and selling a clever carved comb decorated with fancy dyes and varnish, but we couldn't compete with the Shantel magically.

Oh, well.

It was time to move on.

The distraction had helped me compose myself, anyway.

I was walking away when I overheard the words *Obsidian guild*. They hadn't recognized me, or there would have been more shouting, and I knew better than to give myself away by visibly reacting. I discreetly kept my attention on the merchant who had spoken, even as I pretended to stop at another booth.

"I don't know all the details," the merchant said. "All I know is they were involved. They set fire to the Shantel trade stall in Midnight's market. They must have been working with Midnight in some way, or else they would have been picked up by the guards right then for disrupting trade. The Shantel stormed off before I got any more of the story—well, I suppose they had no reason to stay, what with all their goods going up in smoke. Long story short, hopefully they'll have more of those combs next time I go north to market. They might cost a little more," the merchant warned, "since the Shantel lost profitable wares in that fire."

My blood ran cold, in a way that had nothing to do with the rain.

Others had drifted closer, drawn by the gossip, and I let myself join that crowd.

The Obsidian guild was the serpiente boogeyman. While it was certainly true that we lived outside serpiente law—my bag was proof of that—it would have been physically impossible for us to be responsible for every crime the serpiente laid at our door. We were blamed for everything from sick sheep to missing children. Every disaster that befell the serpiente people was put before us, added to a constantly growing tally of unforgivable crimes.

We had been actively hunted ever since the serpiente queen, Elise, had died in a fire. Her three-year-old daughter, Hara, had cried arson, and on the basis of that child's hysterical testimony, every member of the Obsidian guild was suddenly guilty of treason.

This time, though . . .

I had helped set fire to the Shantel market stall. I had done so with their blessing, to make a pyre for the dozen blackened, rotting bodies of human slaves, who had been collateral damage in a Shantel plot to murder the masters of Midnight. The corpses had been piled on the Shantel stall as evidence of their failed treason.

I was one of a very few who knew how close the Shantel had come to succeeding, and what part our guild had actually played in the plot. Malachi, Vance, and I had breathed in the acrid stench of charred blood after magic slew the Shantel witch responsible—the witch *we* had encouraged to take the attack one step further so he could destroy Jeshickah herself. I had feigned ignorance, of course; we all had. Miraculously, Jeshickah had believed us. Her continued belief in that lie was essential to our survival.

I listened long enough to confirm that the current rumor, while unflattering, was no more dangerous than the dozens of crimes of which we had already been convicted.

According to the serpiente, we were bloodtraitors in fact if not by law; we had betrayed our own kind, and were working for the vampires. Rumor said that the Shantel had attempted to fight Midnight, but we had turned them in.

I turned away with my stomach rolling. The merchant, who spoke with the exaggerated drama for which serpiente were famous, made his living trading with Midnight. Yet he called *us* traitors? He probably hadn't complained when the serpiente king sold two of us into slavery less than a year ago.

I returned to the palace gates with my mind heavy but no hesitation visible in my step. I swallowed thickly as I passed the guards, but they saw nothing.

Time to go home.

Hunted, hated ... being in the Obsidian guild wasn't an easy life, but it was a *good* life. I returned to the main camp directly, occasionally pausing to make sure I hadn't been followed, until I passed between two tall fir trees and breathed in the scent of our campfire a little past dusk.

An outsider could have walked through the center of the Obsidian main camp without realizing it was anything but more forest. Even the longhouse, which was large enough for our fifteen members to all sleep there at once—as long as no one wanted privacy or personal space—seemed to blend into the dense evergreen trees and thick, brambly underbrush.

Most of my kin were probably inside now. The sky had

darkened to a dusky purple, and rain was falling heavily enough to make a proper fire impossible outside, so they would have gathered around the longhouse's central hearth to share warmth, as well as the suffocating closeness that serpents always seemed to crave.

I pushed back the oiled skins that served as the longhouse door and was greeted by the heady smell of simmering stew.

"Any problems?" Torquil asked as he extracted himself from the pile of people sprawled in front of the hearth and stood to take the heavy sack of food supplies from me.

Though a simple rat snake, without any of the many strains of power that could be found in our world, Torquil was often jestingly referred to as our "kitchen witch." He possessed the magical ability to turn camp rations into something delicious, even in the latest dredges of winter or now, the earliest bloom of spring, when the nights still tended to drop below freezing and few edible plants were yet available. The stew currently simmering on the hearth smelled like heaven.

"No problems," I answered. "We're being blamed for supposedly betraying the Shantel to Midnight, though."

"Damn." The curse came from Farrell, who had founded the Obsidian guild when he was almost as young as I was now, based on a tribe described in ancient serpiente myths. "I'm sorry, Kadee."

I shrugged. Farrell himself had been accused of

everything from theft to murder to treason and rape—the last being a crime the serpiente viewed as so vile, it did not even merit a trial before execution. He knew what it was like to be vilified for something he hadn't done, without any way to speak up to defend himself.

"We didn't, right?" one of the others asked, sounding half serious. Farrell replied with a glare sharp enough to cut. "Sorry," he said. "If we're going to make the Shantel into another powerful enemy, though, I would like someday to hear the whole story."

"No," Farrell answered flatly, "you wouldn't."

The serpent held Farrell's gaze a moment longer, considering, and then looked at me. "Sorry, Kadee. I know it was bad." He glanced back at Farrell. "I'll trust you. That's all I need to know."

He went back to whittling.

This winter, I had come very close to dying in a cold, dank cell with a bloodstained dirt floor. That cell occupied my all-too-frequent nightmares these days. I had told Farrell the whole story when I returned to the Obsidian camp by the grace of God, and had afterward heeded his advice to keep the details otherwise private, even from the rest of our guild. If the story of our complicity with the Shantel's failed plot ever reached Midnight, we would all be executed, so the fewer people who knew, the safer we all were.

I shoved the sack of supplies at Torquil, then backed out the door. No one chased me, for which I was grateful.

Normal serpiente were never alone. Children stayed with their parents until they were old enough to join communal nurseries. Adults slept in nests with friends, piled on large pillowlike beds without proper form or boundaries, and later took lovers. When distressed, they sought others of their kind and found comfort in the press of skin against skin.

But I was half human, and sometimes I needed to be alone. The other members of the Obsidian guild were the first serpiente I had ever known who respected that decision.

On my way to my own tent, I almost tripped over Malachi, who was sitting in front of the cold, sodden ashes of the central campfire. He seemed to be gazing into a phantom flame only he could see with his pale, blue-green eyes.

Malachi was something like a prophet and holy man and something like an ill relative one takes care of out of a sense of familial responsibility. Despite the damp chill in the spring air, he was wearing nothing but buckskin pants and a dagger at his waist; his shirt, vest, and other weapons lay discarded beside him. His fair skin and white-blond hair looked like silver in the rain, as if he had been carved from precious metals instead of born to a living mother. Glowing indigo symbols writhed across his skin, writing and rewriting themselves on his flesh like slow-moving lightning. Unlike his half siblings, Misha and Shkei, who claimed ignorance of magic, Malachi had undisputed power inherited from his falcon father.

"Hello?" I asked quietly, the way one might call into a darkened room.

Malachi didn't respond. He was focused on the visions dancing behind his eyes. Most of the time, Malachi's trances ended on their own, when he was ready or when he was needed. Over this past winter, though, they had been more common and started to last longer. His brother and sister used to be the most successful at waking him, but Shkei had been gone for almost a year now, and Misha ... *Oh, Misha.* She had been imprisoned in Midnight for months before we had managed to get her back, and her time there had left its mark.

Misha wasn't in the longhouse. She was sleeping in her own tent, with the front flaps closed. That was how she slept every night now.

Twenty-two years ago, Malachi had spoken the prophecy that seemed to define so many of our days: "Someday, my sister, you will be queen," he had said. "When you and your king rule, you will bow to no one. And this place, this Midnight, will burn to ash." By the time I joined them, only three years ago, the guild that refused to bow to any king or priest, and knew no religion higher than day-to-day survival, treated Malachi's prophecy as if it was a holy text. It was why we had done so much, and even sacrificed young Shkei, to get Misha back.

I looked at our prophet, with his gaze lost somewhere in the rain, and at the closed tent where our supposed future queen hid away from the world, and tried to convince myself that I still believed such a future was possible.

CHAPTER 2

OUT OF THE corner of my eye, I glimpsed a flash of green just in time to turn and see Vance return to human form, shaking long, messy chestnut hair out of his face. All the other members of the Obsidian guild were serpiente, but Vance was a quetzal shapeshifter. His bird form was dramatic emerald with a ruby-red breast and two long green tail feathers that trailed behind him like streamers when he flew. In his human form, he was a year younger than I was, only fourteen.

"Hi," I said as he stepped up beside me.

"Are you all right?" he asked. "You were . . . staring."

Just like Malachi, I thought. I nodded distractedly. "The cold," I explained vaguely, shivering. I wasn't quite as susceptible as most serpents to the whims of temperature, but

I was soaked to the skin. What was I doing philosophizing in the rain?

Vance moved closer to me and tucked one arm neatly around my waist, under the cloak. Unlike snakes, birds were naturally hot-blooded, and Vance's body radiated heat like a small furnace. He wasn't technically avian—that title applied to the hawks, sparrows, crows, and ravens who served the Tuuli Thea, while Vance's heritage lay with the jaguars and quetzals of the south, called the Azteka—but his blood ran as hot as any bird's. Hotter, perhaps, because he was by birth a bloodwitch. Though he would never be able to harness that power for his own use, it kept his body warm.

"I didn't know serpents shivered," Vance remarked. Innocently, I was sure he thought.

I shrugged. "I'm special."

"Yeah," he replied. Then he blushed. "I mean, well— I've noticed that you're sometimes ... different. Not in a bad way. Just different."

Sweet and adorable Vance had no idea how that bit of "different" had defined so much of my life. I hadn't yet found the nerve to tell him that my mother had been human, because Vance had been raised in a world where humans could be nothing but slaves. I supposed I would have to explain eventually, because shivering wasn't the only thing real serpiente didn't do. They also didn't sweat. After shapeshifting, they didn't return to human shapes choking down bile and trying not to vomit, as I did when my body returned with slow confusion to its proper form.

Not tonight, I thought.

I had been saying that to myself for months now. At first, I had wanted Vance to know me as a person before he realized what I was. Now . . . I kept telling myself that it was no big secret. The rest of the guild knew. It just hadn't come up yet with Vance. The Obsidian guild had a lot of stories, which Vance hadn't heard yet because he had spent his first four months with us simply learning how to survive in the harsh reality of the wild woods.

For now, we retreated to the diamond shelter where the two of us usually camped out. A large oilskin tarp was pinned down at three corners and propped up by a long staff at the fourth, so we were protected from the worst of the rain and wind but never lost sight of the open air. Neither of us liked to be trapped.

Vance had been with me in that cell four months ago. Before then, he had lived in Midnight for fourteen years, raised to be a lord in that despicable realm.

Now, he was Vance Obsidian, and he was one of the only people I could stand to have so close to me. He made no assumptions, and asked no questions when I needed space.

He turned his back now as I stripped off my trader's costume and changed into the wool, fur, and buckskin garb that clothed us and marked us as children of Obsidian. Warm, practical, and protective, the clothes had been white while the ground still wore winter's snow; now that spring was here, those same pieces had been tanned and dyed so they provided camouflage in the forest.

When I slept that night, my dreams started pleasantly enough.

The fire flickered, sending sparks up to the midsummer sky. On this, the shortest night of the year, the serpiente celebrated with music, dancing, fire, and feast.

I watched and clapped in rhythm as Misha rose on her toes to begin the Namir-da, the ancient dance that celebrates the origins of our kind. She had never received formal training, so she made up the steps with joyful abandon. Her fair skin and diamond-white hair, marks of her white-viper heritage, reflected the nearly full moon.

In the midst of her dance, she reached out to snag Torquil's arm, pulling him up to spin with her in front of the fire. When Torquil's mate, Aika, reclaimed him with a playful scowl, Misha reached for Farrell, the man who had brought us all together.

With Farrell, we had all found a home—we outcasts, traitors, and thieves. We were hunted by the serpiente, by Diente Julian Cobriana's guards, but that was the price of being free. Now, on the longest day of the year, we rejoiced in that freedom.

"Come dance, Kadee," Misha crooned, when Farrell left her to bring another of our clan into the dance.

"You know I'll just make a fool out of myself," I told her.

"Why should that stop you?" She pulled on my hands, lifting me to my feet. "You are a child of Obsidian, and you carry in your veins the blood of the goddess Anhamirak, she who gave us freedom, and passion, and beauty. There is no creature in the world with the right to call you a fool."

She grinned, and spun me around so fast I would have fallen if she hadn't caught me.

"See?" she said. "There is no danger here. Trust me."

Trust me. They said that white vipers like Misha had magic, though she always laughed off the suggestion whenever it came up. I believed it, though. No one else could have convinced me to whirl in front of that fire, trying to recall steps I had only ever half learned as a child in the dancer's nest before they cast me out and I was taken in as a ward of the royal family.

Well, maybe one other.

Shkei returned from the market with two heavily laden bags of goodies he had "liberated" from this or that merchant's stall. If Misha's magic was persuasive, able to convince even a shy girl like me that she could be beautiful—even for a few minutes—Shkei's magic made him invisible, trustworthy, so he could walk through the market where he was wanted for treason and remain utterly unnoticed.

Shkei grinned when he saw me dancing. I blushed, then stumbled. Misha caught my arm and my gaze, and I raised my chin defiantly, daring anyone to judge me.

Shkei knew better. Without so much as a snicker, he passed his bundles to Torquil, dropped his cloak to the ground, and held out a hand to me. *His moss-green eyes sparkled in the firelight as I reached for him.*

That was when the soldiers appeared.

The dream shifted, darkened. Instead of the joy and hope of Namir-da, my unconscious traveled dark paths my waking mind had never actually experienced.

The dark, stone cell. Marble floor, slick with blood—my blood. The collar around my neck was suffocating, too tight to breathe past.

I looked up at the vampire, the black-eyed trainer who had purchased me and whose task was to strip away my individuality, hope, and free will.

He hit me, and suddenly it wasn't the trainer standing there but Paulin, one of the guards who used to serve the princess Hara but was reassigned to be my "honor guard" when the royal house took me in. He blamed me for interfering with his courtship of the princess, and took every private moment to let me know it.

I tried to run, to hide, and tripped over a boy sitting on the floor.

Shkei! Run! *I thought.* He'll kill you if he catches you!

It wasn't Shkei, though. Instead of Shkei's long white-blond hair and moss-green eyes, this boy had dark hair, skin like copper pennies, and eyes the deep green of pine needles. He sat calmly, with a harp in his lap, and played a tune that was mournful and chilling.

"Run," I tried to whisper, but my throat was too tight.

The man behind me—part vampire, part Paulin, some evil

blend of the two–stepped past me and dragged the boy to his feet. The harp fell to the ground and shattered like glass, sending shards into the air that cut my skin.

I woke gagging. Shaking. My insides cramped, my muscles writhed, and I couldn't seem to get my breath.

Seizure, I thought. I hadn't had one in years. I struggled to draw air into my lungs, but I couldn't. I could almost taste the blood from my nightmare.

Calm yourself! I tried to get my body under control, the way the Shantel fleshwitch had taught me when I was seven, but felt myself losing the fight. Vaguely, I was aware of Vance calling to me worriedly, but my eyes had already gone dark.

Firm, rhythmic pressure on my shoulders suggested a slower pace for my breath. As I focused on that, I became aware eventually of a cool, gentle voice.

"You're here with us, Kadee. You're safe with your kin." *Farrell.* He had only seen me this way once, the day Paulin really *had* almost caught Shkei. I had surprised the guard with a knife in the back, taken Shkei's hand, and run to the Obsidian camp with him as if all the demons of Hell were following me. Harming a royal guard was treason, and I had done more than *harm.* Somehow, my desperate blow had killed the man whom Hara Cobriana—heir to the serpiente throne—now claimed had almost been her mate. By the time I had reached this place, I had been in a full panic.

"Stay with me," Farrell said, as if he knew my mind

had turned down another dark, dangerous path. "Listen to the birds and other animals waking in the dawn. Smell the campfire. You are safe here. Think about your breathing, and let it match mine."

I struggled to listen. Around us, I could hear the morning calls of birds. The squeezing of Farrell's hands on my shoulders matched the rhythm he set as he drew each breath in, then let it out with a low whistling sound. I followed that pace with my own breathing, and gradually the black clouds that had descended on my vision parted.

Farrell's gray eyes met mine, calm and controlled, from where he was kneeling in front of me. I held his gaze and we continued to breathe in sync until the cramping in my muscles had subsided and I knew the danger of a seizure had passed.

"Are you all right?"

I nodded, dazed. I looked around, blushing with embarrassment, and discovered that the others were diligently going about their tasks and paying no attention to me except for occasional curious glances, which were quickly averted. I suspected Farrell had told them to give me some privacy. They were doing the best serpents knew how to do with such a command.

The only person who had defied the order was, of course, Vance. His skin, normally a rusty tan, looked gray, and his worried brown eyes were fixed on me.

"Are you all right?" he asked, as if Farrell's question wasn't enough.

"I'm all right," I said hoarsely. "Is there—"

Before I had finished asking, Farrell produced a waterskin. I drank deeply of the stream-cold water, then splashed a little on my face.

"What happened?" Vance asked, kneeling beside me.

Before I could try to form an answer, an angry shout from across the camp caused us all to look up. Farrell sighed and said, "That's Misha and Aika again. I should break it up before they kill each other."

His tone was tired, and perhaps resigned, which gave me the chills. Misha had come back from Midnight with night terrors and a biting fury that unleashed itself upon anyone foolish enough to cross her. Aika was a strong, opinionated woman known for taking down grizzly bears using the blade-tipped stave that was the Obsidian guild's signature weapon. Both were always armed.

"If you're all right, I should probably referee," Farrell said as he looked with concern at the women across the camp.

"I'm fine," I answered, trying to look less exhausted and shaky than I felt. "Go, before something permanent happens."

Serpiente were passionate. Even the best of friends fought sometimes, occasionally coming to blows. However,

if Aika and Misha's ever-escalating fight got any worse, I agreed with Farrell: it would be bloody, and one of them might not survive it.

Farrell took me at my word and went to the two women. I faced Vance, who was still waiting for an explanation with anxiety clear on his face.

I had been told as a child that these fits, legacy of my human heritage, could kill me if I didn't learn to control them. I had discovered for myself that they had damaged my mind somehow, stripping vividness from memories and stealing words. What could I have lost, if Farrell hadn't helped me avoid this one? Would I have opened my eyes to find I didn't recognize a member of our group, or I suddenly didn't know how to find the stream where we got our water? Would I have looked at the boy with a quetzal's feathers in his hair, aware that I knew him but unable to bring his name to mind?

Across the camp, Farrell was physically pulling Aika and Misha apart. Torquil was tensely organizing supplies, and occasionally stealing glances to Aika, his mate, as if ready to jump in to help if Misha drew a weapon. Malachi was gazing at his furious sister, the one who was supposed to be our savior, with a look of guilty horror.

Maybe it would be good to forget. Forget the way Misha used to laugh, and grin, and challenge the world. Forget Shkei, and how we hadn't been able to save him. Forget the years when the Obsidian guild had been a true fam-

ily, and not this fractured, angry group, which seemed held together more by our shared fears and desperation than by kinship.

No, I thought, shaking my head to clear my own cowardly thoughts. *I don't want to forget. I refuse to lose anything else.*

CHAPTER 3

I HAD JUST opened my mouth to try to answer Vance's worried inquiry—maybe not with the *whole* explanation, but with enough that he would understand—when Malachi suddenly appeared beside us, like a rock plunking into a pool.

Vance jumped, but I was so used to Malachi's ways that they couldn't startle me anymore. He embodied the magic that allowed our guild to disappear into the woods, invisible to the serpiente guards who would like to kill us. Unless he made a point to be obvious, the half-white viper, half-falcon prophet could walk through a crowded room without drawing a single eye.

"Morning," Vance said tensely, when at first Malachi simply looked at us as if waiting for one of us to say something.

Malachi blinked twice, then shook himself as if coming out of a cold lake.

"Morning, Vance," he replied. "Are you going to the market today?"

Vance frowned, looking to me with obvious frustration, then told Malachi, "Yes."

Many of our day-to-day supplies came from the serpiente market, or directly from the forest in which we lived, but other needs couldn't be met locally. Midnight's market had the best blacksmith—the only one who would actually deal with the Obsidian guild—and was the only place to find most goods produced by avians, the Shantel, the Azteka, or other even farther-off groups. It was also the only place we could sell any of our own wares.

We visited Midnight's land only when we had to, two or three times a year. We had all been surprised when Vance offered to join the group traveling north this time, in what would be his first return to Midnight's land since he had walked away from that empire four months ago. Some had speculated that he intended to leave us and take the so-called masters of Midnight up on their offer for him to join them. I had spent enough late nights talking with Vance that I had no fear that he would return to that place; he had something to prove to himself, I suspected, and this was how he needed to go about it.

I personally had no desire to return to Midnight's land so soon after our last misadventure.

"Did you want me to look for something for you?" Vance asked, when Malachi's gaze went distant again.

Malachi nodded absently.

"Something in *particular*?"

I bit my cheek to suppress a smile. Sometimes Malachi was perfectly coherent, reasonable, and understandable. He could fight when he needed to, and could be unsettlingly persuasive when he chose to be. Other times, he walked with one foot in a different world. The rest of us were so used to Malachi that we mostly ignored his odd behavior when it surfaced. Vance was the only one who deliberately provoked him.

Maybe that was a good thing. Malachi sucked in a shuddering breath and this time seemed to come fully back into our world. His eyes focused on Vance, then me. He said, "There is something you need there."

"Can you be more specific?" Vance asked.

He's going to look for a new knife for me, I thought, *and Torquil wants salt and cayenne.* I doubted that was what Malachi meant, though, and unlike Vance, I tried not to interrupt Malachi. Sometimes, speaking to him cut off the entire conversation.

"Kadee, what about you?" Malachi asked.

I shook my head. "I'm staying here," I answered, with a little more certainty than I suddenly felt. Malachi had no authority to give me orders, but his visions had guided the Obsidian guild for longer than I had been alive. If he thought I needed to go to the market for some reason, I couldn't just dismiss his words.

Malachi shook his head, frowning, and said, "You need to look for a boy with a harp."

The statement gave me chills, as it brought forward the last image from my nightmare.

That dream had been false—a mishmash of my knowledge and my fears—but the boy with the harp was real, and one of the few vivid memories I had from my childhood. The most terrifying days of my youth had been spent with a Shantel witch determined to make me well, after my seizures had become so severe and so frequent that my human parents had been convinced I was dying. I hadn't understood what the witch was doing, or why, and my fear had only exacerbated the symptoms she was trying to control. The only comfort I had was a boy named Shane, who would sit next to my sickbed, play the harp, and sometimes sing in the lilting, exotic language of his people.

"What about him?" I asked Malachi.

"I don't know," he answered.

"If you don't, then we certainly don't," Vance said sharply.

"Is he going to be there?" I asked, though it seemed unlikely. Shane was prince of the Shantel, one of the few civilizations with the power and arrogance to resist full subjugation by Midnight. Their magically guarded forest had given them the leverage to negotiate with the vampires from a position of strength the rest of us could only dream of. Among other things, instead of sending a prince or king to Midnight three times a year to balance accounts, as other empires were required to do, the Shantel stayed in their own territory and had Midnight send a representative to them.

It wasn't surprising, really, that one of their own had found the nerve to try to fight Midnight.

Midnight would have demanded flesh in payment for that crime. The Shantel, who never traded slaves, had probably bargained for a fine of equivalent value in coins and trade goods. It was what they had always done. Midnight would have demanded a high price for their audacity, but the vampires didn't want anyone to realize how close the attack had come to succeeding, and they wouldn't risk losing face by insisting on a punishment they could not possibly enforce.

All this passed through my mind before Malachi answered thoughtfully, "No, I don't think so."

"Who's the boy with the harp?" Vance asked.

"I don't know," Malachi answered, before I could untangle my thoughts enough to speak. If Shane wouldn't be at the market, why did Malachi want me to go there to look for him?

"What about you?" Vance asked. "Are you coming with us?"

Malachi shuddered, seafoam eyes widening. "Not if I can help it," he replied. "Too many ghosts."

He stood and walked away without another word, and approached his sister, who was sorting and packing her gear with quick, angry motions. Her fight with Aika seemed to have blown over, for now.

As the two siblings exchanged soft words, Vance shook his head and said, "I will never get used to him."

At least Malachi and Vance hadn't argued this time. I preferred Vance's confused annoyance to the tightly wound fury Malachi had triggered in the past. I wasn't sure what had gone on between these two, but in Vance's early days in the Obsidian guild, their arguments had been at least as bad as Aika's and Misha's.

"He's usually less obscure," I pointed out. "Would you excuse me a moment?"

I didn't wait for permission before I stood almost as abruptly as Malachi had.

Farrell was deep in conversation with Aika as I approached. I overheard her saying, "Sometimes I think she *misses* Midnight, with the way she goes on. Are you sure she's not going so she can find an excuse to sell herself back?"

"I can only pray she is not," Farrell said, each word precise.

"And watch your own back. She—" Aika broke off when she noticed me. "Kadee, it looks like Vance will be in charge of the blacksmith trip. I'm staying here after all. Did you still want me to help you with your staff-work?"

I was a fair shot with the bow I carried, and I could throw a knife with reasonable accuracy—at least, before I stupidly lost my favorite in the flank of a deer that fled before I could try for a better shot—but Aika was determined to teach me more defensive fighting skills.

"Actually," I said, looking from Aika to Farrell, "I was thinking I might join the group going to the market."

I expected him to object, even though he believed absolutely that a child of Obsidian was subject only to her own will. Farrell guided but did not rule, and the rest of us often listened but were expected to make our own decisions.

Instead, he raised his brows with surprise. "First Vance, then Misha, and now you?"

"Misha's coming?" That explained why Aika *wasn't*, and what they had been talking about when I approached. "Are you sure that's a good idea?"

If Misha lashed out at someone in the market, she would be arrested by Midnight's guards and end up back where she had been, back where her night terrors made it clear a part of her was still trapped. It would be passive suicide.

Like Aika, I suspected it had crossed Misha's mind at least once that it was easier to give up than it was to be a prophesied savior.

"No, I'm not," Farrell answered. *But it isn't our place to tell her no.*

I swallowed, wondering if I dared go and risk being near her—

No, I told myself. *She has nightmares, and she's on edge, but she isn't suicidal. She is supposed to be the one who will rescue us from Midnight. How can she do that if she is too afraid to even face the market?*

I had to believe that.

"Do you still want to come with us?" Farrell asked.

I nodded. "Malachi said something to me about Shane and the Shantel."

"You still have an open invitation to visit Shantel land, don't you?" he asked. "You don't need to look for them in the market."

I bit my lip. As absurd as it sounded, I felt safer in Midnight's market than I did in the Shantel forest. My "open invitation," as Farrell put it, was left over from when I had been a child. The Shantel were not normally so welcoming of outsiders, but they were the ones who had stolen me from my human kin and brought me to this world of shapeshifters, and it was their magic that had taught me to shapeshift before the seizures killed me. Because they had taken responsibility for me once, they claimed they had a responsibility to me in the future as well.

Despite that noble notion, I wasn't sure my invitation would still be valid. If the Shantel had heard the same rumors as the serpiente, and thought the Obsidian guild might be responsible for turning them in, they might conveniently forget I had once been a child in their care.

"Malachi said I should go," I said, feigning indifference that Farrell was sure to see through.

"As you wish," he answered. "We'll leave in an hour."

The next hour was occupied with frantic packing and rapid conversations about value, and which supplies were most needed and which we should only get if we could afford them. Aika didn't trust anyone but Farrell to negotiate the sale of the hides she had tanned and other tools she laboriously created throughout the year. Those could usually be exchanged for blood coins, mostly from the Shantel, which was why we had planned this trip to coincide with their normal spring trading window.

Torquil had Vance memorize a list of spices and other ingredients we needed, in order of importance. He didn't mince words as he admitted that the Azteka who sold most of those would either give Vance a better deal because he was supposedly related to one of their holy bloodwitches, or they would try to cheat him because he was considered a bloodtraitor. "If they give you a hard time, don't hesitate to remind them that your coins are as good as anyone's, and if they don't believe you, they can ask one of the guards to check."

Vance paled a little but didn't respond except to nod.

We were about to get on our way when Aika pushed a few extra coins into my hands. "Get a better knife this time. The handle on that last one was loose. Take care of

Vance," she added, dropping her voice. "This can't be easy for him. And . . ." She glanced at Misha, as if to check that the white viper wasn't listening. "If there's trouble, you and Vance get out of the way. Don't go jumping into the middle to protect her. You hear me?"

Others might have called it cowardly advice, but I nodded, because it was futile to go up against Midnight, and fighting a futile fight for some idea of honor wasn't our way. Such was the life of the Obsidian guild, my chosen family, which lived and sometimes died by the ideals that no man had the right to rule any other, and that he who lives to run away, *lives*.

CHAPTER 4

"DID YOU KNOW Aika and Torquil are trying to breed?" Misha demanded of Farrell, almost as soon as we had stepped outside the bounds of Malachi's magic, which hid our camp from passersby.

If we looked over our shoulders, we wouldn't see or hear the camp, but that didn't mean they couldn't still hear *us*. I could picture Torquil restraining his mate to keep her from coming after us.

"I know they want a child," Farrell replied blandly, replacing Misha's coarse wording with something less . . . *Less like Midnight*, I thought. *Midnight talks about breeding people as if they were horses or dogs.* "I also know they were trying to keep it quiet until they were successful," he added, with a touch of censure in his voice and a nod toward Vance and me.

I hadn't known, though I wasn't exactly surprised. Ser-piente didn't find marriage or monogamy as important as humans did, but Aika and Torquil had declared themselves mates well before I had ever met them. It seemed natural enough that they would want children.

Misha shook her head. "It's ridiculous, not to mention selfish," she huffed. "This is no life for children."

I saw Farrell flinch, and remembered that he had once been a father. His mate, Melissa, had shared Misha's opin-ion. After Naga Elise's death, when the first accusation of treason had fallen on Farrell, Melissa had left the Obsidian guild and begged sanctuary from the serpiente king, Julian. She had brought Farrell's child with her, and when she had become Julian's second queen, her son, Aaron, had become his son as well.

Therefore, the only son of a man who had dedicated his life to the principles of the Obsidian guild was now called a prince. Before I had joined the Obsidian guild, I had known Aaron fairly well. He had treated me like a kid sister, but it was obvious that he was every inch a young man used to privilege, and blind to anyone else's struggles. He had no idea that the infamous outlaw Farrell Obsidian was his father.

"Weren't you born in the Obsidian guild?" Vance chal-lenged Misha. "Would you rather Farrell had left you and you brother where you were?"

"Vance!" I gasped, shocked. If Farrell hadn't bought

Malachi and his mother from Midnight, Misha would have been born a slave of that empire.

"At least Shkei would probably still be alive," Misha mused. This time, I was the one who sucked in a sharp breath, feeling as if I had been struck. "Malachi says the vampires planned to cull him, but my older brother has a knack for survival. He would—"

"That's enough," Farrell broke in. The sharp command, so different from his usual thoughtfully permissive approach, made it clear how deeply Misha's speculation had hurt him.

"Of course, *sir*," Misha replied, turning long enough to give Farrell a baleful glare before speeding her pace so she could once more walk several steps ahead of us.

Farrell sighed heavily, but said nothing. What was there to say?

We reached the boundary of Midnight's land, a bridge over the rapidly tumbling Barri Creek, two long days later. Though the four of us were supposedly traveling together, we were far from companionable. It was difficult to hunt effectively while carrying the amount we were and still make good time, but Vance and I used trying as an excuse to range ahead of the others, where Misha's voice couldn't reach us. Farrell stayed close to her, protective, and when I saw how tense and drawn he looked in the evenings I felt a twinge of guilt, but mostly relief that I had avoided her seemingly poisonous voice.

We approached the bridge at sundown. Most serpiente traders would have camped for the night in the clearing on this side, which was maintained for just that reason, then moved on after sunrise to reach the market by midday, but we paused only long enough for the sun to duck behind the trees before stepping onto the trade road.

This was one of the most dangerous moments of our trip. The trade road was the most likely place for us to run into other serpiente, and on this side of Barri Creek, we were likely to be shot without warning if we were recognized by their guards. Unfortunately, the "creek" had high cliffs on either side and wide rapids at the bottom, so crossing at any other point was even riskier.

Midnight was the only local empire that didn't consider us outlaws or worse, which meant we were technically much safer in their land than any other, as long as we didn't overstay our welcome. We could travel in Midnight's forests as long as we were intending to trade, and their laws protected us from the other shapeshifter nations who would like to see us dead. However, the penalty would be swift and severe if they judged we were actually *living* here. The only shapeshifters allowed to do that were the ones who officially worked for the vampires' empire, and they were even more despised than we were.

More than we used to be, anyway, I thought, remembering what I had heard in the serpiente market. Midnight didn't consider us employees—bloodtraitors, as they were referred to by other shapeshifters—but the rest of the world seemed to be leaning that way.

We finally reached the market midmorning. As always, the sight of the guards at the gates made my hackles rise. The men and women in Midnight's burgundy regalia were here to make sure the vampires' laws were being followed, which meant they were the ones ensuring we could trade here safely. . . . Still, it was hard for me to trust any guards, much less ones I knew had chosen to leave their own people to work for Midnight.

Normally, the guards made an attempt to avoid conversation unless there was a problem. They knew that most of the merchants and shoppers here considered them traitors. Today, one of them noticed Vance, straightened, and greeted him with a respectful "Sir."

The acknowledgment made Vance flinch and freeze at the threshold of the market. Misha was standing with her shoulders tight and her nostrils flared, like a horse on the verge of bolting. Farrell and I exchanged a concerned glance.

"You don't need to come," Farrell said. "The two of you can camp farther back, and Kadee and I can do our trading."

"I need to," Vance answered, taking a determined step forward as if pushing his way through the memories this place evoked. I knew that Vance had status in Midnight—I had heard Jeshickah's offer to let him stay as one of them—but it was hard to reconcile that knowledge with the young man I had come to know the last few months. We feared these guards because they represented the vampires' empire. It was disturbing that *they* seemed to fear *Vance*.

I followed Vance's lead, and our movement seemed to break Misha out of her paralysis. She followed without a word, and we passed into what Midnight claimed was the greatest market in the world. I wasn't sure I believed that, but it sprawled larger and offered more luxury goods than anywhere I had ever seen or expected to see in my life.

The exchange of sundries like food staples, simple spices, leather, fur, and iron made up only a small fraction of this market's trade. From far to the south, the Azteka brought exotic pigments, feathers, stones, raw silver, cocoa, and sugar. The serpiente were known for their fine dyes, wool and flaxen fabrics, and paper and ink. The avians had the best metalworkers; I intended to visit their blacksmith about a new knife, but their real business here was in gold and silver, and fine ceramics. Shantel merchants could quite literally work magic with leather, fur, bone, wood, and other natural items, though most of those items were far too pricey for the likes of us. More often, they sold carved or sewn items ranging from practical tools to useless decorations.

This market, surrounded by waist-high stone walls and policed by Midnight's guards, showcased the best that the shapeshifter nations had to offer. The *best* of the best went to Midnight itself, in exchange for the two basics that empire had to sell: freedom, and food.

Farrell caught my eye, looked pointedly to Vance, and then nodded to Misha. The communication was clear—he would watch out for Misha, and I should keep an eye on Vance. The quetzal's pace slowed every time he passed a guard wearing Midnight's uniform. I couldn't imagine what thoughts were going through his head, but I was proud of him for facing this fear.

I stepped closer to Vance, silently saying, *I'll stay with him.*

"We need to see the Shantel," Farrell said to Misha.

We had intended to split up here, but Malachi's words prompted me to say, "We'll go with you."

Beside me, I felt Vance tense, and I regretted my words.

"The boy with the harp is Shantel?" Vance guessed, his tone carefully neutral.

Vance's history with the Shantel and their magic was at least as tangled as the one he had with Midnight. Without Vance's knowledge, a Shantel witch had infected his blood with a spell that made it poisonous to vampires in a bold but ultimately unsuccessful assassination attempt. I didn't want to force him to face more than one demon from his past at a time.

"Do you want us to ask about Shane for you?" Farrell asked, immediately recognizing my quandary, and offering a solution.

I nodded. Shane probably wasn't even here. "We'll meet back up after Vance and I see the blacksmith," I suggested.

The smith's shop was one of the largest permanent structures in the market. The Mistress of Midnight's love of horses was well known, which meant a farrier was always expected to be in residence.

Misha quirked a brow. "The Shantel will not like having a child of Obsidian inquire after one of their princes," she pointed out.

We were hardly a threat to the Shantel, but that didn't mean they would take such questions kindly.

"The worst they can do is refuse to answer," Farrell replied logically. "They can't refuse to trade."

Among the serpiente, rape was a high crime. Among the avians, familial abuse was considered one of the worst offenses. Among the Shantel, there was no trespass more vile than disrespect of the *sakkri*, their high priestess, prophet, and conduit to their magic. But in Midnight, nothing was more holy than trade, which meant the only unforgivable sins were those that undercut the bottom line.

"Impeding trade" was punishable by fines up to the value of the trade, and Midnight's choice of payment was always flesh. As long as merchants continued to fear slavery more than they hated us, they would never refuse to trade. Not here, inside these stone walls.

CHAPTER 5

"WE MIGHT AS well stay together," Vance said, his voice soft but determined. With obvious false bravado, he added, "Malachi's a prophet, right? Who am I to second-guess his guidance?"

On second thought, maybe it wasn't bravado I heard, but irony. The look he shot at Farrell in that moment wasn't friendly, as if he wanted to pick a fight.

"I trust Malachi's vision," Farrell answered patiently, "but even I acknowledge that his words are often unclear. The Shantel's treatment of you was intolerable, Vance. They used you as a weapon without ever asking your consent or considering your safety. If you want to face them, come with us and we'll stand with you, but there's no shame in turning your back to them if that's what you want. As for words of prophecy . . ." He shrugged. "You're a child of Obsidian now. You can let prophecy guide you if you choose, but even fate is not your master. Do whatever your own conscience says you must."

That was our creed, the one the Obsidian guild had always followed, but Vance seemed deflated by it. It was as if his anger had been holding him up, protecting him from his fear of this place, and so he lost a little strength when Farrell refused to argue with him.

I wanted to apologize for putting Vance in this position, but I would have been doing so to make myself feel better about my careless words, not to comfort him. I bit my lip and stayed silent, leaving the decision to him.

Vance sighed, shook his head, and said, "In for a penny, in for a pound."

He started forward, leading the way toward the Shantel. As I followed, I couldn't help but remember the last time we had come here together: the stench of corpses killed in the plague the Shantel had intended for the vampires; the heat of the pyre; the taste of adrenaline and despair at the back of my mouth.

When we reached the area where the Shantel normally traded their wares, we found only a darker patch of earth and the heavy, lingering stench of ash.

"Did we miss them?" Misha wondered aloud. Unlike the avians and serpiente, who maintained a fairly constant presence in the market, the Shantel visited for a couple of weeks at a time only a few times a year. We normally timed our visits to coincide with theirs, but it was certainly possible to show up a few days early or late; I had assumed that was what happened to the merchant who wanted to buy their bone combs, but now I felt a chill running up my spine.

"Have you seen the Shantel this season?" I asked a nearby merchant. Out of the corner of my eye, I watched Vance drift into the middle of the burned patch. In his mind, was he here—or was he back in Midnight? Was he thinking of the Shantel or the vampires?

"Not since the fire," the merchant replied. "Midnight hired a crew a while back to clean up the wreckage. I heard them saying the cost was being added to the Shantel accounts."

"It's been four months," I said, more from shock than protest. "Farrell, are the Shantel that self-sufficient?"

The serpiente and avians couldn't survive without Midnight, but I wasn't sure about the Shantel. Their magic could keep the vampires from storming their land and taking their people by force, but they could still starve.

"I don't think so," Farrell answered. "They used to be, but their population has grown since they've been trading with Midnight."

Vance, meanwhile, had engaged one of Midnight's

guards. After a brief conversation, he returned to us with a frown and reported, "Midnight is offering a substantial reward for any Shantel captured and brought to them, and the guards are under orders to arrest them on sight if they show up here."

"I think my brother sent you on a wild-goose chase, girl," Misha observed. "He probably saw some vision of when you were a kid and confused himself."

Farrell, as usual, tempered Misha's caustic words with his own logic. "Malachi does sometimes get timelines confused. He might have been thinking of a future visit. Or perhaps—"

He grabbed Misha's arm at the same moment that I looked back up at the empty space that had been the wreckage . . . and found myself staring into familiar garnet eyes. My blood ran cold. My heart raced. Every muscle in my body quivered, preparing me to flee. I felt my companions go still around me. Even Vance apparently recognized Hara Kiesha Cobriana, heir to the serpiente throne.

The first time I'd seen her, I was seven years old. I had never met another serpiente, and I feared that she might be a demon. Her black hair and blood-red eyes had terrified me. I hadn't seen Hara since I was thirteen years old, and now, that old horror crept in.

For what seemed like an eternity, we were all frozen: me, Farrell, Misha, Vance, Hara, and the serpiente guards behind her. The shapeshifter nations weren't allowed to keep a standing army, but they were encouraged to have guards to police their own people.

With one hand still holding Misha's wrist, as if concerned she might bolt, Farrell put his other hand on my shoulder. He gently turned me away from Hara as he whispered, "Look over there."

Over there was the guard Vance had spoken to a moment ago. *Midnight's* guard. He was watching our tableau with sharp attention, one hand at the hilt of his sword.

Remembering that even the heir to the serpiente throne was helpless here, I let out the breath that had been locked in my chest. Hara had probably come to review her accounts . . . though that wasn't a comforting thought either. A balance on Midnight's sheets would mean soldiers in our woods, like the ones who had taken Misha and Shkei last year.

That last thought made me so angry that I turned back to Hara without fear of her royal power or her red gaze. "Move along, cobra," I said as boldly as I dared. "There's nothing for you here."

Farrell squeezed my shoulder in what was probably meant to be a warning. We were safe here as long as we didn't start a physical fight—which would get us hauled in for disrupting trade—but antagonizing the royals still wasn't necessary, or wise.

"We should go," Farrell urged us. "Just—"

"Run?" Hara suggested, her tone cutting. She took a

step closer. Her gaze flickered to Midnight's guards—others had drawn near now, intrigued by the sight of two enemies squaring off—and I saw her pointedly move her hand away from the dagger she wore at her belt. Softly, so she wouldn't be overheard, she hissed, "Please do. I would love to continue this conversation more privately." Her eyes scanned our group, and then she added, "I see one white viper who should be in Midnight's cells, but I don't see your witch Malachi. I doubt you can slip out of sight as easily without him."

Misha lunged forward with a curse, and Farrell and Vance only barely managed to hold her back.

All I kept seeing were these soldiers grabbing Misha and Shkei, on what was supposed to be the holiest night of the year. Misha was certainly reliving those memories, too, along with ones far worse than I could imagine.

I couldn't keep my mouth shut. "How do you sleep at night?" I demanded of Hara. "You claim to stand for a nation that worships freedom. How do you justify selling a sixteen-year-old boy into slavery to pay *your* taxes?"

The royal house was known for its temper, and Hara would have struck me if her own guards hadn't restrained her.

"It helps that I have better bedfellows," Hara snapped, shaking off her guards' hands. "I'm not beholden to a murdering rapist." She glared at Farrell. "Or the bloodtraitor who sold out the Shantel." That was directed at Vance.

Then she turned back to me. "Then again, your hands aren't exactly clean. I would love to believe the white viper bewitched you, like legends say they can, but he never could have convinced you to commit treason if you hadn't already let him in."

"We leave *now*," Farrell hissed. "Misha. Come on. Vance. We need to—"

"They can't assault us here," Vance said, stubbornly holding his ground as Farrell tried to herd us away. "I'll leave when our trading is done. I won't let them chase us away. Besides, I'm curious about what I supposedly did to the Shantel. Care to enlighten me, Hara?"

She responded with incredulous laughter. "Are you trying to claim *ignorance*?" she asked. "You're standing beside the man who murdered the serpiente queen—my *mother*, incidentally—the girl who murdered my would-be mate, and a woman who would be in Midnight now if the vampires hadn't oh-so-conveniently released her. You're keeping company with the guild that abducted Alasdair, princess of the avians, and sold her to Midnight. Are you really going to pretend that you are innocent?"

Vance blanched before saying simply, "Excuse me?"

My whole body chilled, in a too-familiar way. When I had been a child, that sensation had preceded seizures.

"We didn't murder Naga Elise!" I protested, uselessly and perhaps even more damningly, because every other accusation the cobra made was true ... and Vance, quite obviously, hadn't known most of it. I had thought that Malachi might have told him about the hawk, Alasdair, but that had obviously been wishful thinking.

As for Paulin, Hara's supposed would-be mate, I hadn't spoken to *anyone* about him since I had joined the Obsidian guild. As far as I could tell, his death had elevated him to a far higher place in the princess's esteem than he had held in life, a fact I knew well since he had blamed *me* for his failure to make any progress in his attempted courtship. My entire life as a ward of the serpiente king had ended in blood, but I wasn't the heartless assassin Hara described.

I don't know what would have happened if Midnight's guards hadn't decided that this had gone on long enough. They broke up the argument, pushing us apart and demanding, "Do you have *business* here?" They were asking the same question of Hara's group.

"Yes," Farrell answered instantly. He lifted the goods we had brought with us and handed them over for inspection. "We intended to trade with the Shantel. That's why we were asking about them. What is their situation?"

"We'll buy your wares," the guard replied. "Who else do you need to trade with?"

"The Azteka, if they're here," Farrell answered, "and the blacksmith."

The guards consulted each other, and then they gave their orders.

"Make your trades quickly—then *leave*," they said.

"The princess needs to tend to her accounts, which will take time, and then she plans to travel east to the Shantel. We will ensure that *all* of her people go that direction, so none can stay to follow you back to your camp." They had obviously heard Hara's implied threat, and intended to ensure that Midnight's laws keeping us safe on their land were enforced even once we left the market. It was odd to realize that, in this place, the Obsidian guild was considered *more* trustworthy than the serpiente.

"I thought trade with the Shantel was forbidden," Farrell commented.

"It is," the guard replied, "but the serpiente are in good standing, so their travel is not restricted. They are bringing no trade goods with them, and are aware of the consequences if they violate trade sanctions."

Emboldened by that response, I asked, "I was planning to try to reach the Shantel as well."

Farrell shot me a long-suffering look. Not only did we have no such plans before that moment, but he was specifically barred from trespassing on Shantel land. It didn't matter; I didn't need his consent. I wanted to know what was happening with the Shantel—Shane in particular—and I had more reason than most to believe I might be allowed into their land so I could assuage my curiosity.

The guards, however, looked skeptical. They were obviously about to deny me permission when support came from an unexpected quarter. "*We* were planning to, she means," Vance said, gesturing to himself and me. "While Farrell and Misha returned to the camp."

Vance was one of us these days, but he had once been highly ranked in Midnight, and the empire's guards still seemed uncertain as to his authority. They weren't going to argue with him. I wanted to do so myself—Vance had been afraid to even set foot in the market or approach the Shantel stall, so why was he offering to go with me? But I would save my questions for later.

"In that case, you two should go now," the guard told us, "before the royal party begins traveling that direction."

Another added, "If you're planning to try to collect the bounty, you can bring their people here or directly to Midnight proper." My stomach rolled at the casual assumption that we might be going to Shantel land to find someone we could sell. Like Hara had said, we were far from innocent, but our crimes had never been about greed. I had never needed coins so badly that I would trade in flesh to get them.

I didn't bother to argue with bloodtraitors, though. Their perception of us was surely part of the reason Midnight would block trade to the Shantel without blocking access. The vampires didn't need to get past Shantel magic, if they trusted that someone else would do their dirty work for them.

There was no more time for discussion. We redistributed our supplies quickly, and Farrell gave me his knife with a whispered plea to be careful, since I hadn't yet been able to replace my own. Then we started out to the east, with the serpiente royal party behind us, and the unknown Shantel woods before us.

CHAPTER 6

"THANK YOU FOR helping me," I said to Vance as we set out on the road that led east from Midnight's market toward Shantel land, "but I understand if you do not want to go any farther. I know you're no fan of the Shantel." Vance had no reason to care about the people who had bewitched him, then sent him back to the vampires like a gift of poisoned wine. They had surely expected him to die, after he passed their disease on to the immortals.

Vance shrugged, his expression distant, lost in thought.

"We don't know what the Shantel think happened," I warned. "If they think we betrayed them, I can't promise we'll be greeted warmly."

Vance and I were the only people alive who had seen four of Midnight's infamous trainers lying, cold and still as corpses, on the stone floor. We had been present when the Shantel witch responsible for poisoning them had been killed by an Azteka woman seeking to keep Midnight's wrath from falling on her own people. That woman never knew we had just infected Jeshickah, and that if she had stayed her hand Midnight's leader would have been destroyed. Since we didn't dare share the real story, it made sense that other shapeshifters apparently thought we had somehow betrayed the Shantel.

Shantel magic was supposed to be powerful, especially when it came to prophecy and knowing about events they had not witnessed. I hoped, even if they thought we had worked with Midnight against them, they would let us speak and would have some way to confirm our account. But I couldn't guarantee that.

"If you're worried, why are you going?" Vance asked at last.

"Because . . ." I trailed off. I couldn't articulate the horror I had felt at the end of my nightmare. I didn't even want to *think* about it. Instead, I said, "Malachi said to look for the boy with the harp. His name is Shane, and he is one of the Shantel I once knew. Malachi wouldn't have mentioned it if it weren't important."

Vance didn't respond, but now my own thoughts were swirling too fast for me to take note. It had been years since I had seen Shane. Back then, I had been a sick, terrified child, and he had been a sweet young boy who had tried to comfort me. Now I was an outlaw, accused of—*guilty* of—

treason against the royal house of the serpiente, and Shane was a prince.

Was I being a fool, putting myself in his land?

The sound of the shattering harp and the stink of burning bodies pervaded my memory, as if to say, *What choice do you have?*

We were almost in Shantel land when Vance broke his silence, and said, "Tell me about Alasdair."

God help me, I thought. I had been so focused on my immediate concerns, I had actually forgotten how Vance had reacted to Hara's accusations.

"I trust you to tell me the truth," Vance added, when I was quiet too long. "That's why I volunteered to go with you."

"I ... We ..." I tried to gather my thoughts. "A few months after Misha and Shkei were sold to Midnight, a mercenary came to us. She said a hawk had crossed one of Midnight's trainers, and he wanted her. Midnight's laws include a clause that says that shapeshifters can't be made slaves unless we disobey those laws, or our own kind sells us in ... so he couldn't take her, legally. Not unless someone ... other shapeshifters, like *us* ... sold her to him."

Repeating the tale with Vance frowning at me left a foul taste in my mouth. The rest of the story seemed obvious enough, so I didn't say it aloud. *We agreed. We sold her, and we got Misha back in return.*

"I met her, you know," Vance said, once I had stopped speaking. "Gabriel owns her, or did when I was there."

"He's the one who asked us for her," I answered softly. "He had Misha and Shkei, and was willing to make a trade."

Vance winced. "Do you have any idea . . ." He trailed off, speechless. Farrell, Malachi, and Misha all did the same thing when they tried to describe Midnight, as if words were not sufficient to express what they had seen within those walls. My own brief glimpse last winter had been enough to sate any curiosity I might have had.

"We believed," I said, "if Gabriel was trying so hard to get her, then he would, whether or not we helped. We couldn't save the hawk, but we had a chance to save one of our own."

Only one.

"There are two of them," I remembered protesting, when the mercenary had offered her deal.

"There is only one hawk. Choose."

Shkei was younger, sweeter, innocent. I would have chosen him in a heartbeat if I could have, but there had been the prophecy to consider. How could Misha bring about Midnight's fall if we let the vampires break her as a slave?

Farrell, as ever, had refused to order any of us. Instead, he had us vote blindly. Twelve had voted to bring Misha home. Only two had voted for Shkei. I was one of them; I didn't know who the other had been. It didn't matter, because as the mercenary had said, there was only one hawk.

"Trainers are good at convincing you of things like

that," Vance said. "That's their *job*, their existence—to get you to believe that there's no reason not to sell your soul, your freedom, your faith, anything that makes you alive and free. They convince you that the blood is there for a reason, a *necessary* reason, and—" He broke off, coming to an abrupt stop.

Ahead of us, the road disappeared. We had reached the edge of Midnight's territory, and the beginning of Shantel land.

"If he wanted her, he would have found a way to get her," Vance said, gazing at the wild forest ahead of us. "You're right about that much. But with the deal you made, he didn't just get a hawk. He got all of you. All of *us*."

"That's not—"

He cut me off with a sharp look, and the words "Isn't it?" Vance verbally reviewed what he had observed. "The serpiente already thought of the Obsidian guild as traitors and criminals, and now the avians and the Shantel and I'm sure others do as well. Malachi rescued his sister, but don't you see how much he hates himself for that? Farrell says Malachi's prophecy is why we're doing all this, but have you noticed that he and Malachi don't even look each other in the eye anymore? And you . . . if you weren't ashamed of it, you would have mentioned it before now. How many nights have we stayed up talking? You never told me about Naga Elise, or—"

"We didn't kill her!" I snapped.

I wasn't even born when Naga Elise, the serpiente queen and the mother of Julian Cobriana's only daughter, Hara, died in a fire. During my time in the palace, I had heard servants say the fire had probably been an accident, but Hara insisted that someone had started it. Some of the servants thought that the child might have caused the fire herself. An accident, surely, but children weren't always able to admit to accidents.

"True or not," Vance said, "what reason have we given *anyone* to doubt our guilt?" He took a deep, shuddering breath, closing his eyes.

I reached instinctively for his hand. His fingertips brushed mine, but then he pulled away.

The accusing tone dropped from his voice as he confessed, "If it hadn't been for the Shantel magic against Midnight, I would still be there, blithely believing everything the trainers told me. Believing order is needed, a few to rule, and many naturally meant to be ruled over. Believing the blood and pain and all the ways they use to 'teach' their subjects obedience are necessary. Sometimes I look at us, lost in the forest, and I want that order back. I want it so badly, I have to put all my energy into running the other direction." He wrapped his arms around himself as if he was cold. "I had almost convinced myself that I had gone far enough. I could even stand to face the market, because Midnight didn't have any power over me anymore."

He didn't have to complete the thought aloud: *I was wrong.*

"I'm sorry," I said. "We should have told you about Alasdair." Vance hadn't asked, and none of us had wanted to share the moment of our lives of which we were all most ashamed. We would all say that we had only done what we needed to do, maybe even that we had done the right thing, but that didn't mean we were proud of it. We had stalked the hawk for weeks, learning her movements. We had learned who she was and who she cared about so we could use that against her in order to capture her.

"I should have guessed," Vance sighed. "I saw the way she responded to Malachi in Midnight."

"You don't have to come with me," I blurted out. "You don't owe the Shantel anything. You shouldn't risk yourself for them."

"I'm not doing it for *them*," Vance asserted sharply. He drew a breath, and his voice was gentle again when he said, "When I went back to Midnight this winter, you came with me. I was still practically a stranger to you then, but you didn't make me go alone."

"I should be safe," I said. "I have—"

"An open invitation," Vance interrupted. "I know. Have you ever gone?"

I shook my head.

"I don't know the whole story," Vance said, "but if you

didn't dread this place, you would have visited at some point."

"The forest might not even let you in," I admitted. "Will you be able to find your way back to camp if we get separated?"

Vance nodded. Not long ago, the quetzal hadn't been able to find his way out of a tree without help, but he seemed to have an innate sense of direction that had quickly developed once he had been exposed to the wider world. Maybe it was a bird thing. Personally, I missed city streets and town markets, like the ones that haunted my dreams and my faintest memories. I loved the forest, but sometimes I wished I had a *road,* literally as well as metaphorically.

We moved forward together, crossing the boundary from Midnight's land into the enchanted forest that belonged to the Shantel.

The woods here seemed simultaneously darker and brighter than they should have been. The light cascaded through the trees in a way that had no rhyme or season. Shadows fell without regard for the location of the sun, and plants that were just peeking up above the ground in other areas were already in full bloom here.

I had lived with the Obsidian guild long enough that I could normally navigate a forest comfortably. I habitually took note of the direction of the light, and which trees marked a straight path. In Shantel territory, however, that didn't work. North wasn't north, and one could walk in a line forward and end up making a circle.

"Where are we going?" Vance asked at one point.

"Hopefully, the Family Courtyard," I answered. "That's what the Shantel call their village. We won't reach it until tomorrow, though."

"Do you have any idea where we are?"

I shrugged. "We're in the forest," I answered. "If we keep traveling, we *should* reach our destination, unless the Shantel don't want us to. We'll be under guard before we get there, if we aren't already." Just as the forest could decide to let us in, send us away, or drive us lost in circles, it could bring Shantel guards to us. "For tonight, the only thing we need to worry about is avoiding the serpiente. We probably got here hours before them, but time and distance in the Shantel woods change, so they could catch up with us."

We traveled until dusk, then set up camp and divided the night into two watches. We wouldn't see the Shantel unless they wanted us to, but we would hopefully hear the serpiente royal party if they approached.

Vance took first watch, and I succumbed to uneasy sleep.

Monsters surrounded me.

I didn't know where I was, or what I had done to deserve this. I was the child of a Patriot in the Continental army and a nurse he had met during the war. They loved me, but what value could I possibly have to anyone else? I was seven years old, and constantly ill. Why would anyone want me?

69

I cried out for my mother, for my father, though my throat was parched and hoarse. They didn't come. Instead, a woman approached me whose skin was dark like clay, and decorated with black and indigo inks.

She spoke to me in a language I didn't understand, and offered me foods I didn't recognize. Some settled well in my stomach, soothing my hunger, but others inspired vivid hallucinations and made my body heavy. They came in bowls carved with symbols that writhed and made my eyes ache when I looked at them.

Sometimes the woman—the witch, I was sure—would leave if I tried to refuse her tonics and potions, but other times, she would call for help. More strangers would come, and would hold me in place so she could force the foul brews down my gullet.

I thought I remembered others coming to me, who spoke English and tried to explain what was happening, but their visits were hazy.

Sometimes Shane was there. He never spoke to me, just played his harp. Sometimes he sang, in that strange language. His music was the only thing that calmed me in this terrifying place.

CHAPTER 7

A WORDLESS CRY of alarm snapped me from dreams to full alert. I reached for my dagger, only to find my wrist caught by shadows in the forest.

I lashed out instinctively, driving my shoulder into the chest of the person restraining me as I tried to stand. Instead, I found myself off balance, with my wrists pinned behind my back by warm hands.

Warm. These weren't serpiente. If they had been, Vance would have seen them sooner, and we would have run. The fact that they had been able to sneak up on us meant they were Shantel.

Vance let out another protest, and I called, "Don't resist! They won't hurt us."

I wasn't *entirely* sure about that, but I didn't have time to say, "As long as we're given permission to speak to the royal family, we will probably have a chance to explain ourselves. If we can convince their leaders we didn't conspire against them, they won't hurt us."

As soon as I stopped struggling, the figures around me became solid, no longer formless shadows. Shantel guards took my bow, quiver, and knife. They were all held by a man whose dark skin was marked with swirls and dots of ink that I recognized as Shantel marks of power.

"We won't hurt you," the witch said, echoing my words. "We have been instructed to bring you to the temple. We cannot do that while you are armed."

The Shantel recognized what they called "three-times-three" types of magic, and of those, eight were common forms that any Shantel could study. Each of the eight paths filled a particular niche in Shantel society: craftsman, explorer, trader, healer, et cetera. I did not know the meaning behind the specific symbols this witch wore, but if I'd had to make a wild guess, I would have said "hunter."

When he referred to the temple, however, I knew he was talking about the ninth witch: the sakkri, a woman dedicated before birth and past death, and revered by even the king.

"No," Vance said, bluntly, as if we still had any power over the situation.

I understood his feelings, but the guards had already taken us by surprise and seized our weapons. What choice did we have but to go along with them? At least the sakkri would probably be able to divine the truth about our role in the plague.

The witch who had taken our weapons explained, "The sakkri herself has demanded your presence."

"Vance," I said, trying to reason with the wide-eyed fear I could see on the quetzal's face, "the sakkri is the person most likely to know we—"

"The last time I was in the presence of a Shantel witch," Vance interrupted, pushing ineffectively against the guard gripping his arms, "he turned me into a plague-bearer so I could murder everyone I cared about before probably being put to a messy and painful death. I came here to support Kadee, because she was *worried* about you people. I do not want to visit with your high witch."

"I'm afraid," the hunter said, "that you do not have a choice. Your weapons will be returned to you if and when the sakkri declares that you are not a threat."

"Are the other serpiente in these woods?" I asked, worried. The last thing I wanted was to run into Hara Cobriana while armed with nothing more dangerous than a wooden spoon.

"They have been sent home," the guards assured me. I lost my balance as my arms were abruptly released. "We'll take our leave now, and see you soon."

Before we could reply, the Shantel faded back into the woods.

Vance spun about, looking for the guards. Even their

footprints were gone now. The only evidence they had really been there was the absence of our weapons.

"See us soon?" Vance asked.

"They already disarmed us," I said, shaking my head. "They don't need to drag us along with them and deal with our arguments and struggles. They trust the forest will put us where the sakkri wants us, regardless of our wishes."

"Are they right?" His tone said he already knew.

"Probably," I answered reluctantly. "Likely enough that we might as well pack up and get it over with. They wouldn't have stepped in to take our weapons if we weren't almost there."

I turned to start packing up our camp, and Vance followed suit. The process didn't take long, and as we finished, Vance asked, "When you said you had an open invitation to visit the Shantel, I guess I thought that meant they saw you as a friend. What do I need to know before we walk into this?"

"Shantel don't really see anyone outside their own kind as a *friend*," I admitted. "I think they see me as a . . . a responsibility. I was a child when I was here last. They promised me I would always be allowed to return if I had a need, but I've had no desire to do so."

I could see the curiosity on Vance's face, but I didn't want to go into detail when I was sure the Shantel guards were still standing nearby, probably close enough to see and overhear us.

For the rest of our trip, our escort remained mostly invisible, only noticeable as occasional shadows in the corner of my vision. I caught sight of the witch again as we approached the low stone wall that marked the edge of the Shantel village. His gaze was on us, but he made no attempt to speak to or restrain us.

The woods did not end here, but they thinned slightly. Cobbles took the place of dense underbrush, and younger trees had been trimmed away, while statuesque red cedar and fir trees still dotted the sprawling, winding space. The buildings looked like they, too, had been grown from the forest. Stone walls blended into clay brick and then natural branches and bark, supplemented with thatched or woven curtains or roofs.

As we stepped past a break in the wall, the other guards appeared around us, forming a corridor I had no doubt led directly toward the sakkri. Outsiders were not permitted to wander Shantel land without an escort, but this was extreme.

"This is the Shantel Family Courtyard," I explained to Vance, trying to fill him in on crucial information while ignoring our armed companions. "If someone here says 'the Family,' they mean the *royal* family. Unless they've had a birth I don't know about, that means King Laurence, and the two princes, Lucas and Shane."

"Big courtyard," Vance observed, with a quirked brow. "No women in the Family?"

"I'm not sure what happened to the queen," I answered. "I know King Laurence married and had children when he was older than usual, so she may have been older, too. They had no daughters, but even if they had, the boys still would have been ahead of her in line for the throne." With a shrug, I added, "I wouldn't be surprised if the magic selects male offspring for the royal family. They have a family tree posted on the wall of the receiving room, going back generations, and it's heavy with men."

"Huh." Midnight was ruled by a woman, and the serpiente believed a woman was as capable as a man, so this was Vance's first exposure to a patriarchal system.

"Their sakkri, the high priestess, is always a woman," I added. "I think they believe the male king and female priestess provide balance. Or something."

I heard one of the guards cough in response to my vague, dismissive description. Somehow, I couldn't find it in myself to be concerned that I had offended him.

Though I knew all three Shantel royals, I had never met the sakkri, with her gift of prophecy. The Shantel's most sacred witch was chosen by the land itself, and recognized at birth by the "white curse," a mark visible on both her human and animal forms. In order to maintain her tie to the magic of the land, she was never given a name. She could be claimed by no one; even the woman who gave birth to a sakkri would never claim the infant as "hers." A sakkri had no parents, no lovers, no friends.

No wonder they call it a curse, I thought.

"The deathwitch said the sakkri sent him to Midnight," Vance remarked, his tone as controlled as if he were discussing the weather.

I didn't know any words powerful enough to soothe him, so I reached out and squeezed his hand instead. Vance shot me a grateful smile, and I tried not to let him see my anxiety.

There wasn't time to say more before we reached the temple, which was a low, round building whose doors were covered by an elaborately embroidered tapestry. Cowrie shells sewn against the fabric had become leaves in an elaborate tree, whose trunk was made of wooden beads, each carved with a different design. The green-and-white shells sparkled in the dappled light.

I forced my feet to move forward, and my hand to reach for the curtain. I smelled the rich aroma of incense and beeswax candles as we stepped into the antechamber. Vance and I both stopped with our toes barely past the threshold, leaving as much distance between us and the two women who seemed to be waiting for us as possible.

"This is a surprise," one of the women said. I was startled to see that she couldn't have been much older than I was, though she was clearly the revered sakkri. Her skin was a deep plum-black, and the "white curse" was visible as markings throughout her long, jet-dark hair. The white strands made striking streaks of silver in the black tresses.

"Liar," I grumbled. "A half-dozen goons showed up to fetch us."

"Did they," said the sakkri. It was not a question, though it was accompanied by a pointed glance to the other woman.

I knew there could be more than one of any of the other witches, but the Shantel always spoke as if there was only one sakkri. I was looking at evidence that my impression was wrong, however, because the second woman also had white markings. She was older, though her face had a timeless quality to it that made it hard to tell her age. Her skin was red-brown, except for the milk-white markings visible along one side of her face like a tiger's stripes.

"Yes," Vance said. "So tell us what you want."

The two sakkri did not look offended by our bluntness. They looked serene. I wanted to say or do something extreme, to break that calm the way they had broken mine.

"We were coming to Shantel land willingly," I snapped. "To *help.* Was a show of force really necessary?"

"We were not convinced you would come to *us,*" the older sakkri said, with a glance to her . . . friend, guardian, mentor? I had no idea what relation to each other these two might have. Either way, the look said that this subject was a contentious one.

"My sister insists that you can aid us," the younger sakkri said.

Sister, then. The white curse was not inherited, and

the age difference between the two women suggested the relationship was ceremonial, not literal. I said, "And yet you claim our visit was a surprise."

"We were not certain if our message had been received, or understood," the older woman said. "You have a connection to our magic from your time here as a child, but it is tenuous. We also tried to reach the white prophet, but he is . . . unreliable. Even if our message was received, we had no way to know if you would respond."

I thought about my dream, and Malachi's garbled words. The dream-image of Shane had gnawed at me, driving me here in a way that I now realized was more than simple memory and concern. *If I had realized it was a deliberate message,* I thought, *I probably* wouldn't *have responded.*

"Who gave you the right?" I demanded, unable to bite back my fury when I realized they had manipulated me magically. "I am *not* one of your people! I'm—"

"*You* gave us the right," the younger sakkri answered, her voice rising with as much hostility as mine. "If it were not for your interference, the exile's crimes would never have been blamed on our people. Midnight would not now be demanding *payment,* not in coin but in our flesh and blood. We—"

The older sakkri placed a hand on her sister's arm, and spoke over her in cool, controlled tones.

"There is no point in our arguing guilt or innocence," she said, quieting the younger woman. "All we ask of you two," she said, "is for you to carry a message. I am aware that you were endangered without your consent by the exile's scheme, but I am also aware that you eventually chose to ally yourselves with him, and actively assisted him. In that way, you are more culpable than we."

Slyly, the younger sakkri suggested, "We could perhaps ease some of Midnight's wrath were we to share that information."

"But we will *not*," the older woman snapped. "Our king has forbidden it. He sees you as an ally despite your rather tarnished reputation. If you will assist us, we will not betray you."

A chill went down my spine as I watched the two sakkri glare at each other. Surely, this kind of dissent in the temple, where Shantel were supposed to look for guidance, did not bode well. I had been sure the sakkri would be able to explain to the Shantel that we were not the guilty party here. I hadn't realized they would spin it the way they had, putting the blame on us regardless of our intentions.

"What is the message?" I asked. I didn't plan to go to Midnight proper—and who else could they possibly need to communicate with?—but there might be a way to pass information to someone in the market.

"Prince Lucas will explain," the younger sakkri said. "They are ready to receive you now, and you are ready to hear what they will say."

I didn't feel ready to hear anything the royal family

might tell us, especially given the way the sakkri had all but threatened to turn us over to Midnight as criminals if we refused to help with whatever it was they needed.

"Let's go see the prince, then," Vance said, with a slight quaver in his voice that suggested he felt as trepidatious as I did.

The sakkri nodded, giving us permission to leave but apparently not intending to come with us. Had we been asked to see them just so they could threaten us?

If this was the welcoming committee, I was not looking forward to the main event.

CHAPTER 8

OUR ESCORT HAD fallen back slightly by the time we left the temple, but unsurprisingly, no one offered to return our weapons before we went to see the king and princes.

The Family's receiving room was pretty in the same style as most Shantel buildings, built into the forest instead of in competition with it. It was hard to tell which parts of the buildings were growing and which had been constructed, where evergreen canopy ended and manufactured roofing began. Breaks in the walls and ceiling let in ample light, but I couldn't help but wonder how they kept out the rain and the cold in worse weather.

King Laurence was an elderly man, with old scars marking the side of his face and streaking the back of one hand.

Prince Lucas, Laurence's older son, was by Shantel law and tradition the day-to-day ruling power. The king was only involved when the prince felt uncertain about resolving matters on his own or when someone questioned his judgment. When we entered the receiving chamber, Lucas was standing beside his wooden throne, as if too anxious to sit still.

Shane, Laurence's younger son, paced behind his father and brother. His closed-off expression made him seem older than I knew he was, and the knowledge that the sakkri had used my warm memories of him to manipulate me into coming here made me even more unsure about how to greet him.

As Vance and I approached, the guards flanking us bowed. I did not. I also did not step forward or offer a hand to shake, though I knew that touch was considered essential to communication among the Shantel. Refusing to touch someone in greeting was generally equivalent to spitting on them.

The way Lucas's eyes blazed when he saw me, however, made me realize I was right not to attempt a friendly greeting. Instead, I stopped as far away as I could without our needing to shout at each other, and Vance followed my lead, lingering just behind my left shoulder.

"Kadee," Lucas said, with a flat, unwelcoming tone that made me shiver. "We did not expect you. Who is your companion?"

Vance spoke for himself. "Vance Obsidian," he said, "formerly Vance Ehecatl. I don't work for Midnight anymore, and I don't work for you, so stop with the ceremony and feigned surprise and tell us what you want from us so we can leave."

Silence fell like a hammer.

At last, King Laurence sighed and said, "Please, be seated."

There were two chairs set up, somewhat closer than I wanted to get, and naturally somewhat lower than the chairs available to the royals.

"No," I said immediately. "Thank you," I added, in a belated attempt at basic courtesy. The sakkri had suggested that Laurence at least had protected us and refused to betray us to Midnight. I didn't want to antagonize him more than I needed to.

"The fact that you carry the name Obsidian does not require you to be contrary," Lucas snapped.

"Your king sits on a dais, and you two stand on a raised platform," Vance said. "We came here to *help* you, but first you threaten us, and now you ask us to sit at your feet. We are not your subjects, and we will not be manipulated."

"Your upbringing is making you paranoid," Shane suggested, his voice kinder than that of his brother's. "We just asked you to sit, not to worship."

"The position says enough," Vance replied, "so I will respectfully stand."

"Please," Laurence said softly, "do not make this harder than it already is. Sit or stand as you like."

Vance stayed where he was. Shane's use of the word "paranoid" probably wasn't much of an exaggeration. Even without considering the harm done by the Shantel themselves, Vance had been raised by individuals who had subtly manipulated him at every turn. He was naturally cautious as a result, which meant I was going to have to be more reasonable.

I was the one who was habitually argumentative, the trait Lucas had assigned to all members of the Obsidian guild. I tried to rein in that impulse, reminding myself that the sakkri were at least partly right. We hadn't willingly involved ourselves in the attack on the trainers, but we had committed ourselves to it. I hadn't fully understood the situation, but I had made up my mind: given an opportunity, I had been willing to risk my life to strike a blow against Midnight.

I hated the fact that the sakkri had manipulated me but the king had defended me. I owed them the courtesy of an open ear, at least.

With an effort at civility, I said, "Let's begin again. Allow me to introduce Vance Obsidian. As children of Obsidian, you know we will not call you king or bow to commands, but as neighbors we will attempt to stand patiently and listen to a request. I'll even refrain from commenting on your sakkri's veiled threat to sell us to Midnight should we refuse, if you give us a reasonable reason to assist you."

Laurence shook his head with what looked like disappointment. Shane stepped down from the dais with what appeared to be a chastising look over his shoulder at his father and brother, and offered his hand to me.

"Thank you," he said as I took his wrist in what I hoped I correctly remembered was a friendly greeting. It had been a long time since I had lessons in Shantel etiquette.

He had shadows under his eyes, and when he mirrored my grip and pulled me forward to hug me, I could feel the exhaustion in his body. He explained, "Our land has been barred from all visitors since we heard about the bounty that Midnight is offering for our people. We have been discussing different options, and the sakkri told us to wait here for her final decision this morning, but I . . ." His voice broke for a moment, and his gaze flickered away from mine. "We did not realize she intended to bring you. That is why your visit is a surprise."

"I can honestly say we wish we did not need to involve you," Laurence said.

"Everyone keeps saying that," Vance remarked, "and yet you seem determined to do it."

Shane turned toward the quetzal with fury in his gaze. He did not offer his hand to Vance but retreated to the dais with tense steps.

"You two act like you are the put-upon party," Lucas snapped, grasping Shane's shoulder as he passed. Shane shook off his brother's grip and returned to pacing. "Believe me when I say you are the last two people I would ever have chosen to help us. You are—"

"They are the ones the sakkri sent," Laurence interrupted his son. "Recall what we were told. They are not as guilty as circumstances make them appear."

"*She* might not be," Lucas cut in, gesturing to me, "but what about *him*?"

"Shut up, both of you!" Shane snapped, his voice cracking on the second word. "You would bicker until this forest *burns*." Shane turned to us again and cut to the point with no regard for authority or protocol. "We need you to deliver a message to Midnight. More specifically, we need you to make a deal."

I had guessed this was coming, but I still didn't understand. "Why *now*?" I asked. "It's been four months."

Lucas drew himself up, pulling in a long, slow breath as if to compose himself. When he spoke again, his voice was heavy with frustration, but he was at least no longer snarling in anger. "Midnight wouldn't even tell us the extent of our supposed crime," he said. "They said slaves had been killed, and that we were responsible, and they demanded payment. For weeks, we exchanged offers, incentives ... threats. We insisted that we had no part in the exile's actions. For over a month, we bickered, before the sakkri divined the truth, that the vampires themselves had been threatened. She says the trainers were nearly killed?"

He sounded incredulous. I had seen it and still barely believed it, but I nodded.

"When we realized they would not accept our protestations of innocence, we offered payment in coin and goods well beyond the value Midnight assigns the slaves. It would have indebted us for a decade, easily."

Unlike the serpiente and avians, who had come to this land as refugees, utterly dependent at first on the vampires for food and shelter, the Shantel had occupied this land centuries before the vampires had arrived to build their monstrous empire. They had never been forced into the crippling spiral of debt that held the other shapeshifters hostage generation after generation.

"And in reply," Vance said, "they cut off your trade and offered the bounty on your people."

"Our last messenger never returned," Laurence said. "We waited weeks and heard *nothing*. Then, about a week ago, one of Midnight's mercenaries delivered a message. Since we have failed to offer acceptable payment . . . they intend to burn the forest." His voice at the end was small, as if he were saying something obscene. To him, it probably was. Even I was shocked.

Once again, Vance and I spoke over each other, but this time it was clear our minds were traveling completely different paths.

I gasped. "Is that *possible*?" I asked at the same moment that Vance asked, "What are you offering?"

I turned toward him, startled by his words and even more startled by his tone. I knew that look, that posture, that voice, and it wasn't one he had picked up among the Obsidian guild. The conversation hadn't been much different when Malachi had negotiated with a mercenary from Midnight regarding Misha's return.

Shane stepped forward, swallowed, and then said in a clear voice, "It's possible. You being here means the sakkri decided the danger is real, and that we must deal or risk far worse. So . . . I'm what we're offering."

"Shane," Lucas whispered, a single word that seemed full of heartbreak.

But you're so young, I thought.

How young, or old, is fifteen years? Vance and I were both outlaws already. Vance was still only fourteen, but he had seen people beaten, seen them die; he had inadvertently caused dozens of deaths. I had taken a life with my own hands when I was only twelve. We had both known terror beyond anything a child was supposed to know, and were treated as adults by our kin in the Obsidian guild.

But all I could think about when I looked at Shane was the boy who had played a harp and sung to me as the flesh-witch's spells and potions rearranged the very fiber of my being, twisting my innards in an ongoing attempt to shove unwilling muscle and sinew into a sleek serpent form. The witch, the Shantel's version of a doctor, had been convinced that if they could just help me change shape once, everything else would fall into place and my symptoms would subside.

I couldn't speak, but Vance could and did. "What else?" he asked bluntly. "When Midnight thought the Azteka were guilty, they demanded one healthy shapeshifter for each dead slave, or one bloodwitch for every ten. In the end, there were over twenty dead—and that's *without* factoring in the price of rebellion itself, including an attempt on the lives of Mistress Jeshickah and her trainers. They won't accept one younger prince for the full price, especially after so much time has passed."

"You sound like one of them," Lucas said bitterly.

"That's why we're *here*, isn't it?" Vance snapped in reply. It was, obviously, which meant I had to let Vance speak even if it gave me chills to hear him talking like a mercenary.

"They have already executed the witch responsible for the crime," Laurence asserted. "A witch whose actions were not even condoned by the Family. And though I hate to admit it, I fear they have probably taken Amber—our messenger—as well. They can't . . ." He trailed off, unable to complete the statement, which he had to know was so optimistically naive: *They can't possibly ask for more than this.*

"His actions were condoned by the sakkri," I said, trying to remember that these people before me—especially the young man so close to my own age—were not entirely innocent. They feigned ignorance, but they were the rulers of this realm. An attempt to assassinate the leaders of

Midnight could only have been made with their consent, or if they turned a blind eye to it.

Of course, if the plan had worked, they wouldn't have been considered culpable; they would have been hailed as heroes. Did that make them martyrs now?

Shane sat at the edge of the dais. He didn't look up, didn't meet anyone's gaze as he spoke.

"Everyone knows Midnight is seeking slaves with magic," he said flatly. "I personally have little magical training, but every Shantel has the same potential for power regardless of bloodline. It doesn't need to be awakened with obscure rituals like the Azteka. That makes me more valuable than any bloodwitch."

Except for the few hitches in his voice, he made the speech coldly, stating facts that he had obviously considered carefully. His brother looked away, as if he could not stand to keep his gaze on the young man who had so coldly assessed his own value and prepared to sacrifice himself.

"Just out of curiosity," I asked, "did you three draw straws? Or was it just the younger son's lot to sell himself to slavery?"

"I made the decision," Shane said.

"I offered myself," Laurence said, "but Shane rightly pointed out that Midnight is unlikely to accept a man past his prime, whose ruling power has already passed to his son. I cannot do the value assessment as rationally as my son, but I do know that one broken-down king will not make Midnight's *point.* Equal value is the excuse. The truth is they want us to hurt."

"What's your excuse?" Vance asked Lucas.

The prince flinched. "The sakkri will not allow it."

"Which one?" I wondered aloud, recalling the way the two women had argued in front of us.

I hadn't intended to offend anyone—this time—but the three men reacted as if I had slapped one of them. It was Shane who finally bit out, "The sakkri speaks with one voice. Her power passes from one mortal body to the next as she meets the needs of each generation, but there is only one."

"There are clearly two." *Stupid,* I chastised myself for being so tactless. They were obviously describing something mystical, and my words were apparently heresy . . . but if the women were *arguing* with each other, they were clearly not "one voice."

"The sakkri may live for centuries, but she is born as a helpless infant, as we all are," Laurence said, with the same long-suffering tone I remembered from frustrated teachers in the serpiente dancer's nest. "She must come of age before her full power manifests. We are at a cusp right now, as the sakkri's new form has just come into her power, but her old form has not yet returned to the forest."

I decided it was time to stop asking questions, though I had a few, like what happened to the older sakkri once the younger one was ready to take over, and more importantly, whether or not they agreed on Shane's plan. I didn't think they did.

I didn't think *I* did.

Midnight would value Shane's pretty face, but not the mind and heart that had prompted him to sit for hours with a hurting little girl. Everyone else had argued with me, *telling* me not to be afraid. That I was fine and safe. Shane had known better. His instincts had told him that I needed a friend, but wasn't able to tolerate one yet.

"If you are all in agreement about this deal," I asked, "why do you need us?"

"We need a neutral party to negotiate for us," Lucas explained. "If Shane goes to propose this deal, they could claim him as they did Amber and still demand more, and he would have no leverage with which to barter. If you speak for us, Midnight will need to agree to terms before . . ."

"Before it can get its hands on the merchandise," Vance concluded, when Lucas's voice hitched and silenced. "So what do we get?"

"Vance!" I protested. His earlier words had been blunt but practical, regarding what Midnight would or wouldn't accept from the Shantel. This was going too far.

"They want us to go to Midnight proper for them," Vance snapped at me, and for the first time, I saw the genuine fury in his eyes. I heard an echo of the words he had spoken to me the day before: *I could even stand to face the market, because Midnight didn't have any power over me any-*

more. I was annoyed with the Shantel, but I couldn't help responding to their desperate situation. Vance was terrified, and that made him angry. "They want us to make a deal. Mercenaries don't work for free, so if that's what they want to turn us into, I want to know what's in it for us."

"Excuse me," Shane whispered, his composure finally breaking. As he turned, walking swiftly from the room, he said, "I've done my part. My father and brother can see to the details."

The door slammed behind him.

CHAPTER 9

LUCAS WATCHED HIS brother leave, then turned on us with renewed malice in his tone. "You act like we're insulting your honor," he spat. "You're already mercenaries—your whole guild is. You get free passage in Midnight's markets, and an open invitation to walk in their halls, because you're bloodtraitors from the start and all the way through. You've betrayed the serpiente and the avians, and now you expect *us* to trust you? Half your guild was created by Midnight, and the other half scurries to do their work as if—"

"Enough!" Laurence interrupted his son with a shout. "The Obsidian guild has never hidden its loyalties—or lack thereof. Will you drive them away for being exactly what we need?"

I knew I shouldn't care what these people thought of me, but Vance's words were still raw in my mind—*What reason have we given anyone to doubt?*—and Lucas's and Laurence's words stung more than they should have. I couldn't resist trying to defend myself.

"Everything you hear about the Obsidian guild comes to you through the serpiente royal house," I said. "It is skewed by their perspective."

Lucas drew a slow breath, as if struggling to get his emotions under control. "I'm willing to believe that *you* are guiltless, Kadee," he said, "and I understand why you think you owe that guild loyalty, but if you truly believe your chosen cohorts are all blameless victims, then I pity you."

Vance shot me a look that said he knew perfectly well we were all far from innocent, but I should let the point drop for now. To Lucas, he said, "So we return to my original point. If we're mercenaries, what do we get out of this deal?"

"What do you want?" Laurence asked with a sigh, a hand on Lucas's shoulder halting his retort.

We don't want to do *this,* I thought, but Vance's critical gaze cut me off just as the king's gentle hand had silenced his son.

"What terms do Nathaniel and Acise get?" Vance asked.

Nathaniel and Acise were two of Midnight's vampires. They were the faces those of us outside of Midnight saw most often, because they brokered the deals, and handled the messy job of transporting soon-to-be slaves. Nathaniel had taken Misha and Shkei off Diente Julian's hands, when taxes were due and the serpiente came up short. Acise had bought Alasdair Shardae from us.

When Lucas spoke again, his face had assumed a porcelain quality. His expression and tone were carefully composed. "Midnight's professional mercenaries are given free passage through the outer portions of our land, and permission to travel—escorted—as far as the Family Courtyard if they have business here. They also share Midnight's rates at our markets."

The deal wasn't anything special for us. Vance and I already had free passage in Shantel land or we wouldn't have been here. I didn't understand what Vance was angling for, but the thoughtful caution on Lucas's face suggested he did.

"The same should apply to all of our guild," Vance asserted.

That could be useful, since Shantel land bordered serpiente land. Free passage would mean any child of Obsidian being pursued by the serpiente could cross the border and hopefully escape. I still didn't think that was Vance's primary goal, however.

Lucas and Laurence exchanged a look, but then Lucas nodded. "If you agree to this," Lucas said, "Midnight will hold you to the laws regarding its employees. You lose legal status as one of us, instead of one of them. Do you know what that means?"

My eyes widened as I suddenly understood. Midnight's laws said that shapeshifters were freeblood unless sold by their "own kind," but the rules were vague on what "own kind" meant. One kind of shapeshifter was as good as another to the vampires, which was why a group of serpiente had been allowed to sell a hawk that the vampires couldn't otherwise legally acquire. Midnight's employees, however, didn't count. Bloodtraitors didn't get to call serpiente, avians, Shantel, or anyone else their own.

Vance wasn't trying to get a trade advantage, or freedom to move in the forest. He wasn't content to know that he personally would never choose to engage in slave-trading; he was making a deal to ensure the choice could never be offered to us again.

"I understand," Vance answered.

"Kadee?" Lucas looked at me. "Is he able to negotiate for your entire guild?"

"No single individual can speak for the entire Obsidian guild," I admitted, "but . . ." I ran what I knew of Midnight's laws through my mind. Given the purpose of the deal—to deliver Shane—and the fact that Vance himself was negotiating it, I was sure Midnight's vampires would recognize the terms as binding regardless of what the other children of Obsidian thought. "On behalf of myself and our guild, I will agree to the terms."

What would Farrell think? Would he be relieved, as I was? The deal with Alasdair had been nasty, soul-sucking business, which none of us ever wanted to repeat. On the other hand, if we had made this deal with the Shantel a year ago, we wouldn't have been able to save Misha.

Perhaps that would have been a good thing.

"Then we are agreed," Lucas said, looking to both of us. Hostility gone from his tone, he added, "Thank you."

Vance said, "I will do my best to negotiate for you, but I cannot promise Midnight will agree."

Lucas stepped forward, and Vance reached out his hand. They clasped each other's wrists while remaining at arm's length, Vance copying the way I had greeted Shane, though with more tension in his stance.

"Kadee should stay here," Vance added, "to ensure Shane does not run."

"He won't run," Lucas said.

Vance shrugged. "I believe that, but Midnight won't." I almost spoke up, but Vance looked at me with an expression I couldn't read. If it was fear I saw on his face, then why was he *going*, much less alone? Or was it anger? "And anyway, I could use some time alone."

"Be careful if their trainers try to help you 'understand,'" Lucas cautioned. "I don't approve of the actions your guild has taken, but trainers have a way of distorting facts to their own benefit."

"Trust me, I know," Vance assured him.

"I suppose you do. Word was, Jeshickah considered making you a trainer," Lucas said. When Vance just nodded, eyes unreadable, Lucas asked, "Do you know how she gets her trainers?"

"No."

"She purchased each of them, just like any slave," Lucas explained. "If she decides she still wants you, she will go to Farrell Obsidian. The deal you just made won't protect you—either of you—from your own guild. So watch your back."

Vance shuddered. "That is the second most terrifying thing I've heard today."

I wanted to speak up, to say that Farrell wouldn't do that to any of us, but my mouth felt full of paste. I trusted Farrell to the end of the earth, but Lucas's warning didn't just include him, and there were others in our guild I wasn't so certain of.

Vance glanced at the window. "The light's still good, so I might as well get on my way. Can I have my weapons back?"

Lucas nodded and gestured to one of the guards in the back of the room, who handed over Vance's and my weapons without asking questions.

"Vance—" I caught his arm as he slid his knife back into place. I didn't like his taking all his fears and doubts to that place. Like Lucas had said, Midnight's trainers would love to put their own spin on any doubts Vance brought to them.

"I'll let them call me a mercenary," Vance said, "but I

won't *be* one. I'll help this once if it means I'll never have to do it again. But that doesn't mean I want you to see it."

Without a farewell, he changed shape, freeing himself from my grasp. The brilliant green and red bird, with its long tail streaming behind it, took to the air and slipped through the open window with ease, leaving me behind.

Stupid bird! I thought with frustration. I didn't care about his pride; he shouldn't go to Midnight alone, and he *knew* it. Chasing him wouldn't help, though, not when I was on foot and he was on wing.

Lucas raised a hand again, this time to summon a woman who had been waiting by the door. She had olive skin and mahogany hair, and I recognized her immediately. Her name was Marcel, and she was a wanderwitch. She had once explained to me how her magic drove her to roam far from these lands, exploring, seeking new places, new people, and new knowledge.

That was how she had found me eight years ago—a half serpiente girl, living in a human town, with human parents.

"Marcel often acts as escort when outsiders come to our land," Lucas said, as if I weren't staring at my "escort" as if she were a particularly gross spider. "I suppose it is an added boon that she is familiar to you already. She will see to it that you have anything you need while you're here."

"Vance was just making an excuse to get rid of me," I pointed out. "I don't really need to stay here, and a prolonged absence may make my guild come looking for me."

And I do not want to talk to this woman.

"You do need to," Lucas replied, "because it was a condition of Vance's assistance. Ignoring any of those conditions is sufficient reason to invalidate any deal he makes. I'll send a messenger to your guild, letting them know we have engaged your services."

This whole world talks like Midnight, I thought. *Conditions, deals, and values placed on things–and people–that should be priceless.*

I needed to push. I couldn't help it. That perfect, judgmental poise, especially after his earlier shift from venomous to patronizing, sparked my fury. "You mean the deal to sell your younger brother into torture and slavery?"

His only visible reaction was a slight narrowing of his eyes. Softly, he warned me, "It would not be difficult for me to confide to the serpiente guards at what place and time you might emerge from our forest."

The threat was enough to silence me.

"Go," Lucas commanded. To Marcel, he said, "She probably isn't dangerous, so she may go where she likes, as long as she is escorted. She will need access to Shane."

"Yes, sir," Marcel replied, her voice absolutely neutral. I wondered what was going on behind her eyes, which were a green-gold color that seemed to catch and reflect the late-afternoon light. Did she know about the deal? Did she know why I was here? Was she not allowed to question her prince, or did she just not care?

Once outside, I didn't know where to go. I *wanted* to go back to the Obsidian camp, but that wasn't an option. Why had Vance insisted on going alone? Was he really so ashamed that he couldn't stand for me to see him and would rather face the vampires on his own? Or was that just an excuse, and he was still angry with me about Alasdair?

Did he, like the Shantel king and prince, believe the worst of Farrell and the others? Did he believe what Hara said about Elise?

Did Farrell really have the previous Naga assassinated? Why would he?

He wasn't a murderer, and there was no imaginable benefit for our guild. And if somehow he *had* been involved, it must not have been the way Hara told it. There had to be another side to the story, just like there was when I killed Hara's guard to protect Shkei, and like there was now, with the whole world thinking we betrayed the Shantel.

It's not your crime to bear, I told myself, ignoring the sudden guilt that cut at me as I recalled the relief I had felt when Jeshickah declared us innocent and blamed only the Shantel for the plague in Midnight. *The Shantel planned their treason without regard for anyone else who might get hurt. They were willing to sacrifice Vance. They wouldn't have lifted a hand to help the Obsidian guild if Jeshickah had taken her wrath out on you all. You did what you could. You don't owe them anything now.*

If I told myself I was innocent enough times, would I

start believing it? Or would I just keep seeing Shane's exhaustion and despair? Keep remembering that they could have turned the blame on me and mine instead of taking it on themselves, but they hadn't?

You shouldn't need to do this, I thought to Vance, who was flying somewhere above the trees to a building he hated and feared. If anyone was innocent, it was Vance, who had joined us after all our crimes had been committed. *But please . . . do it well. It is the least we can do for these people, who tried to save us all.*

CHAPTER 10

"THIS ISN'T EASY on Lucas," Marcel said as I hesitated outside the Family receiving chamber, trying to plan my next move. "It isn't fair of you to bait him."

She had heard my bitter words, and Lucas's nasty response. Of course she would defend him. He was her prince; he could do no wrong in her eyes.

"A lot of things aren't fair," I replied bitterly, without giving Marcel the benefit of a proper greeting or even looking her in the face. Some wounds were too old, and too deep. "I don't recall that stopping *you*."

I headed toward the building, which held the common hearth. As long as I was stuck here, I might as well use their food supplies instead of my own. Making a meal and eating it would at least keep me occupied for a while.

"If I hadn't taken you away," Marcel said, matching her

pace to mine, "you would have died among the humans. I was barely able to keep you alive long enough to get you back to our fleshwitch."

I bit my tongue, because I knew she was right about that—*damn it*—but I didn't have it in me to forgive her. She had stolen me out of church while my mother was speaking to the pastor.

"I thought once you met your own people—"

"My *own people*," I snapped, spinning to face her, "were my *father* and *mother*, the man and woman you dismissed like worthless baggage when you took me away. I never even had a chance to say goodbye!"

Marcel drew back in the face of my fury. I expected her to shout at me. I *wanted* her to shout, because a screaming argument would have been so satisfying in that moment. Instead, her expression fell and she sighed. "I am not sorry that I saved your life, Kadee, but I *am* sorry your time among the serpiente has been so hard. I do not know how you fell in with the Obsidian guild, but if it matters, I am proud of you for standing up to them now. I understand—"

"Excuse me?" Confusion and shock twined now with my irritation.

"I've heard the stories," Marcel answered softly. "I know that Malachi and Farrell betrayed us to Midnight. It is very brave of you to come here to help us. It is also understandable that you are suddenly longing for another life and other kinships."

I started to speak up to defend the Obsidian guild, then snapped my mouth closed again as I considered. The royal family had learned of the full situation from the sakkri, but apparently those leaders hadn't felt it necessary to tell the truth to the rest of their people. However, Marcel obviously also assumed I was defying my guild now, probably because the sakkri would never have brought me here if I were a threat.

"You are no longer a child," Marcel continued, as if I weren't standing there flabbergasted. "If all you need is sanctuary and protection from the Obsidian guild, you can find that here. If you truly believe you were better off among humans, than I will invite you to accompany me the next time I travel east. Humans rarely travel far; we should be able to locate your . . . parents. But I ask you to first consider carefully; the life of a young human woman is far less free than the one you have known among shapeshifters."

For a moment, the offer took me completely off guard. Home. I could go *home*.

It's not home anymore, I reminded myself. Home these days was a campfire in the wild woods, surrounded by my Obsidian kin. Still . . . the idea of going home and seeing my parents again was appealing. I imagined standing before my father and telling him, "I remember everything you taught me about kings and freedom and responsibility. I was only a child when I saw you last, but—"

The brief daydream shattered as I tried to imagine

explaining shapeshifters, witches, and vampires to my parents. Would they accept me back, or would they scream and run in horror from a monster?

If Marcel had been right, and I really was *running* from the Obsidian guild, the allure of going back to my human family would have been irresistible. I didn't need to stay forever, but a chance to tell my parents I was alive and they should be proud of me was more than I had ever imagined possible. For now, though, I had responsibilities to the family I had found in this land.

I didn't owe Marcel an explanation, but maybe she could help me with another question that had been needling me ever since we traded Alasdair for Misha.

"Do you believe in prophecy?" I asked.

A wanderwitch wasn't necessarily an expert, but the Shantel culture was rooted in the notion that the sakkri's judgment should be followed without question precisely because of her ability to see into the webs of prophecy. That meant everyone within that world should know a little about magic, right?

"Yes," Marcel answered without hesitation, though she sounded puzzled by the shift in topic. Perhaps she didn't know how much of my life in the Obsidian guild had been guided by words of the future. Even our sins—*especially* our sins—had been committed in the pursuit of Malachi's prophecy.

"And you believe they always come true?" I asked.

"Yes, always," Marcel said, "but they do not always come true the way we expect."

"Then if a prophecy predicts something very important, at what point do the ends justify the means in fulfilling it?"

We had sold Alasdair to save one of our own, but that alone wouldn't have driven us to slave-trading . . . I hoped. Far more important than the life of one person was the fact that Misha was supposed to destroy Midnight. How could she do that, if we allowed it to destroy her?

More hesitantly now, Marcel said, "These are questions that would be better asked of the—"

"I don't want to talk to the sakkri," I interrupted. "I want to know what *you* think."

"Well." She paused, considering my words. "I think you misunderstand prophecy. What is foretold *will* come to pass. Fighting to make prophecy true or false is a fool's errand. On the other hand, as I understand it, these things do not always mean what we think they will. It's . . ." She shook her head. "I'm sorry. I know only as much as any Shantel. If the sakkri gave you a prophecy you do not like, then I suggest that you talk to her."

I frowned, and leaned back against the wall of the Family home. "This prophecy isn't from the sakkri," I said.

"Oh." She immediately brightened, as if that answered the question all on its own. "In that case, concern yourself with the reliability of the prophet, not with the prophecy."

The prophecy around which we had done so much had been spoken by a child who had been judged too mentally unstable to keep as a slave. Jeshickah had sold Malachi and his white-viper mother to Farrell Obsidian for a pittance, after deciding they were worthless to her.

Marcel put a hand on my shoulder, probably intending to be comforting. "If a prophecy is true, what it foretells will come to pass. If it is false, then that, too, will sort itself out. In the meantime . . . will you consider my offer? I do feel responsible for you, Kadee."

I pulled away from her, nodding absently to acknowledge her words. I even managed a rough "Thank you. I—"

I lost my train of thought as I noticed Shane. He was sitting at the base of a tree with his knees up to his chest, his arms resting across them, and his head down. He didn't seem to be crying, but exhaustion and defeat were obvious in his posture.

My preference would have been to back away quietly, but he looked up at us and then beckoned me over, saying, "Come sit with me, Kadee?"

Spending time chatting with the man we were working to sell into slavery was not high on my list of things I wanted to do, but he had done as much for me, once.

Marcel hung back as I approached the younger Shantel prince.

"Vance went," I said, unwilling to be more explicit. Shane would know why. "He told me to stay here."

"To watch me."

"To get me out of the way," I admitted. "He ... isn't happy with our guild at the moment ... or with himself, I think, and the whole idea of going to Midnight."

"I feel the same way," Shane sighed.

I sat beside him, leaning against the wide tree trunk and trying to think of something to say that wouldn't sound stupid. I checked my instinct to jerk away when he reached out and put a hand over mine, on my knee. Shantel touched even more than serpiente. Pulling away would have been cruel.

I couldn't talk about the present or the future, so I reached into the past instead. "I don't think I ever said thank you."

"For?"

I spent so much time feeling angry and defensive that I had never become very good at expressing gratitude. I stumbled over my words as I tried to explain. "When Marcel first brought me here, you were ... kind. In a way no one else was."

"Oh." He smiled, though it had a sad tilt to it. "It wasn't entirely selfless. Your fear gave me nightmares."

"My ... what?" Apparently, he was no better with accepting thanks than I was at offering it.

"Part of Shantel magic is our tie to the land and the people on it," Shane explained. "The royal house has a stronger tie than most, and I have always had a particularly strong ability, even when it comes to outsiders. I can tell you if an intruder crosses the boundary of the Family Courtyard, or if a woman goes into labor ... or if a child in the healer's hut is terrified." He shrugged. "It took years of study in the temple before I could master that magic, and back when you came to us, I was still a child myself. I couldn't block your nightmares from my mind, but music made them go away."

The fact that the act had been partly selfish didn't make it mean any less to me. I was about to say so when another thought crossed my horrified mind.

"Is that ability limited to Shantel land?" I asked. "Or will it happen anywhere you go?"

"To varying degrees, it is the case with any land I am in. Beyond my own people, it happens the most with the serpiente, since they are a somewhat empathic race themselves," he explained. "I sense almost nothing when I visit avian land, because their people are very guarded with their emotions. I have never been to Midnight."

He said the last bit flatly, but it was clear he knew why I had asked, and that the thought had already crossed his mind—probably repeatedly.

I tried to imagine what it would be like to sense the emotions of the scores of slaves inside Midnight's walls. So much pain, terror, and despair.

"Isn't there any way for you to fight?" I blurted out. "One of your witches used Vance to nearly kill every trainer in that building!" His eyes widened, and I saw the warning in them, as if discussing this—even here—was too dangerous. I lowered my voice, but pressed on. "You're acting like you're helpless, but everyone knows how powerful Shantel magic is. You—"

I broke off, realizing that if the Shantel *did* have some plan to fight Midnight, they probably wouldn't want to tell me about it.

Shane shook his head. "Our magic isn't well suited for battle. Even a bladewitch weighs every action against the balance of natural life and death when he hunts for meat in the forest."

"What about a deathwitch?" I asked. The witch who had poisoned Vance's blood had implied that he had power over the vampires because of their strange un-life.

"Among our people, deathwitches prepare the dead for burial," Shane said. "They help souls find their way to the next world, and comfort those who remain behind and mourn. They aren't warriors, or assassins."

"But one of them *did* find a way to fight," I pointed out.

"Ask Rachel about her craft if you wish," Shane suggested. "She is our current deathwitch. Perhaps a child of Obsidian can find a way to plot treason where we law-abiding fools are blind."

If there was a secret plot, I decided, Shane didn't know of it either. Did I dare pursue such a dangerous task myself? The alternative was sitting back and doing nothing.

I had to at least ask the question.

Shane gave me directions to a clearing at the edge of the courtyard, where a woman was sitting, playing a flute. Her eyes seemed focused on the fire before her, which burned inside a circle of stones whose outsides were milky white, in stark contrast with the soot-black sides facing the flames.

The tune was melancholy, which matched my mood, and the serpent in me could not resist watching the hypnotic movement of the fire, the woman, and the instrument swaying. I sat beside her and waited to be acknowledged, watching the way her fingers danced on the flute. Black marks decorated the backs of her hands.

"Who are you mourning?" she asked me as the song came to a close.

"Mourning?" I asked. "I'm sorry. Is this some kind of memorial? I didn't mean to intrude."

I imagined I would always hold some bitterness toward the Shantel, but I would never knowingly intrude on a private ritual.

"You are not intruding," she replied. "You are replying. So I ask you, whom do you mourn? The music would not call to you for any other reason."

"I'm not mourning anyone," I said. "I wanted to talk to you about . . ." I trailed off. Was I really about to tell a complete stranger that I had once been involved in an assassination attempt that had nearly killed Jeshickah herself? And I wanted to try *again*?

The witch's eyes widened slightly, and she said, "I can only hope that his rest is peaceful. I cannot go to that place to help guide him back to our land. I do not think Midnight even buries its dead."

"I think they burn them," I said, my mouth suddenly pasty. She was talking about the deathwitch I had been thinking about. "Can you read my mind?"

"No," she answered, "but I can feel the deaths that you have known, especially when your mind turns to them. Two of your deaths occurred in Midnight's cells."

I frowned. The witch had been the only . . . *"Oh,"* I whispered as I realized who she meant. "Shkei. I wasn't there when he died."

"Your heart was," she answered. "You mourn for him."

"Can you tell me anything about him?" I asked. I didn't really want to hear about my friend's grisly demise at a trainer's hands, but if he had to die alone, how could I shut out the details?

"He wasn't alone," the deathwitch said.

"He was with the trainer, I assume." That wasn't any better.

"No." Staring deep within the fire, she said, "He was with someone who cared about him. Someone he cared about."

Misha? No—she had been back with us by the time Malachi told us Shkei was dead.

"I'm sorry," the witch said. "I know nothing more."

That was fine. Mourning the dead was important, but I would far rather save the living, if I could. "Do you know about the spell the other deathwitch created, to poison the vampires?"

She winced. "Yes," she said, barely a whisper. "So many deaths. I felt them all. I do not know how one of us could have crafted such a poison. It is a perversion of our power to destroy any life, even one we despise."

So much for hoping she would try again, I thought.

"They were all children once, you know," the death-witch said, again looking away from me. "Even the mighty Jeshickah was born human. The trainer known as Jaguar has a blood-sister among the Azteka who cannot help but seek the brother she once knew. The one known as Gabriel is as dark a villain as any of us can imagine, but they say he loves his hawk."

Alasdair. The woman we sold. "His slave, you mean."

"I do," she agreed. "He loves her, nonetheless. But he is broken, and does not know how to love something and let it be free at the same time."

"Are you trying to convince me the trainers aren't evil?" I asked incredulously. With her own prince on the brink of belonging to them, how could she make such a claim?

"They *are* evil," the witch said flatly. "But once, they were children. I cannot prophesy the future, the way the sakkri can, but I can see and mourn what they might have been, if they had not been twisted into what they are."

Can you see who Alasdair would have been, if we hadn't sold her into that place? What about Misha—who would she have been, if she had never entered those stone walls?

I didn't ask. Some questions were better left unanswered.

CHAPTER 11

I TRIED TO conceal my frustration as I returned to Shane, though I realized it was probably futile. What was the point of *prophecy*, of magic, if it did nothing to help us? I was sick of saying "someday, things will be better," but not being able to do anything!

"Your people have spent *centuries* refusing to bow to Midnight," I told him. "You can't convince me they've never threatened you before. How is this time different?"

"Part of Midnight's hold on people is its rigid adherence to its own laws," Shane answered. "As long as Midnight doesn't cross its own lines, obeying the vampires' laws remains safer than standing against them. Submission ensures safety and survival, while rebellion . . . well." He shook his head. "Midnight could never bring its full force against us without breaking its own rules. Arbitrarily crushing us would send a message to everyone else they rule that there is no safety in obedience. It would ensure an uprising."

"But now Midnight can blame you," I said, filling in the blanks. "You struck first."

"So they can strike back as hard as they want," Shane replied. "They cannot afford to back down, not when they say we tried to assassinate the trainers."

"You're really going to go through with this?" I asked stupidly. Did he have any other choice?

"Sometimes, there are fights you can't win." He sighed heavily. "We tried to stall and wheedle our way out of this, and Amber paid the price. She was just a merchant delivering a message, but when Midnight stopped playing around, she was the one within their reach." His gaze slid to me, and I saw the wry acknowledgement in it. "I suppose that's the kind of sin a child of Obsidian expects from a prince. The Family played power games while inside this forest, and let one of our subjects pay the price. We should have protected her."

What could I say to that? *You should never have let one of your people try to fight Midnight.* Or, *You should have rolled over the moment Midnight asked for payment and given them anything they asked.* Those options weren't any better. *You should never have hoped to win.* I couldn't believe that.

If I believed that, everything we had ever done was useless.

"I'm sorry," I whispered.

He took my hand and squeezed it. "None of this is your fault."

But it is, I thought. *If we hadn't involved ourselves, Jeshickah never would have connected the plague with your people. Malachi and I would probably be dead. Vance certainly would be. I am not sorry we chose to stay alive . . . but I am sorry that you are the one who will pay for it.*

Shane shot to his feet and started forward before I realized anything was wrong. As I followed, I began to hear shouting, and recognized Vance's voice. It was too soon for him to have made it to Midnight, negotiated a deal, and returned to us, but he was here anyway, pushing his way past the guards, toward the temple.

"You can't just—"

"Let go of me," Vance snapped at the guards who were trying to restrain him. "Unless you want to discuss the definition of 'impeding trade.' "

Vance's dark hair had come out of its tie and was rumpled around his face, not quite concealing the scratches on his cheek and jaw. Some of them were still bleeding. Those crimson beads brought a sick feeling to the pit of my stomach, as if they portended far worse to come.

The guards, who had hesitated at Vance's words, drew back to let their prince pass.

"What is the meaning of this?" Shane demanded, grabbing Vance's arm before he could storm into the sakkri's receiving room.

"That is what I would like to know," Vance answered. Raising his voice, he called, "Are you in there?"

The older sakkri emerged and looked at Vance, and then Shane. "What can I do for you now, mercenary child of blood?"

Vance frowned at the appellation. "Odd name to give me, when you are the one who is trying so hard to sell your prince into slavery—or so you say. Do you think Midnight is going to be swayed by a ruse like this?"

"What are you talking about?" Shane asked.

"I'm talking," Vance bit out, "about the fact that the forest will not let me pass. It wouldn't even let me above the treetops to fly. It nearly broke my wing knocking me to the ground, and then gave me these." He tilted his head and brushed his hair back. In the light, the cuts and new bruises down the side of his face looked even worse.

I had been worried about him going to *Midnight*. I had never even stopped to wonder if he was safe in the Shantel forest. How many of the Shantel believed, like Marcel, that the Obsidian guild was responsible for their current predicament? How many of them thought Vance and I were traitors?

"The forest answers to the sakkri," Vance said, "so I want to hear what they have to say."

The sakkri stepped forward and reached toward Vance, who jerked back.

"I just want to check the wound," she said.

"Let me," I said, stepping between the sakkri and Vance. It would be a long time before he would let another Shantel magic user put hands on him, even when it was supposedly for his own good.

"It's fine," Vance said, shaking me off. "I want to know why it happened in the first place."

"I am sorry you were wounded on our behalf," the sakkri said. "I did not intend it."

"You, singular?" I asked. "What about your sister?"

"I am certain she did not wish a guest to come to harm either," she responded, "but she is indisposed at the moment, so I cannot ask."

"Is she ill?" Shane asked, the concern in his voice comical. With everything else going on, his anxiety over the sakkri's sniffles seemed overblown.

The older sakkri shook her head. "Sometimes the power speaks very loudly. It can be overwhelming, especially when one has just come into the visions, as my sister has."

"So, if you didn't mean to stop him," I said, interrupting, "and your sister didn't, and the entire royal family is behind this mission, then why wasn't Vance allowed to pass?" A more personal concern struck me. "Are we trapped here now? I'm sure I speak for all of us when I say that if Midnight burns this forest, I do not want to be in it."

"It won't come to that," Shane said, with the absolute certainty of a man who has never doubted his power or his place in the world. "Vance, what exactly happened?"

I remembered Shane's description of his tie to the people on his land, and how he could sense an intruder crossing the border. "Shouldn't you already know?" I asked.

He shook his head. "I love my people, but I have been working very hard *not* to feel the way they do about the current situation. Thanks to years of study in the temple, I can do that ... mostly. I've been sensing their anger and grief for days. If I felt the attack on Vance, I didn't notice it as anything different."

"All I know," Vance answered, "is that one moment I was flying, and the next, something hit me hard enough that I blacked out. I woke up just outside the village."

Remembering the argument we had witnessed earlier, I said to the sakkri, "You and your sister seem to disagree about this plan. Could her magic be overriding yours?" I knew the Shantel men had objected to the idea that the two sakkri might not agree, but surely someone had to recognize there was some dissonance here.

Some of the guards who had run toward the ruckus looked like they would object to my question, but the sakkri answered first. "She does not *like* this plan, but we both understand what we must do to survive. She would not sabotage that."

"*Someone* did," Vance pointed out. "You're damn lucky I'm trying to help you, and not actually on Midnight's payroll. What do you think would have happened if your magic had assaulted one of the vampires?"

There is no luck in the Shantel woods, I thought.

"If our power had turned on one of the blood-drinkers," the sakkri replied calmly, "it would not have brought him, mostly uninjured, to the Family Courtyard. The forest did not want you to leave, but it knows you are not an enemy."

"Stop blaming *trees*," I snapped. Vance already held a grudge, and didn't trust the Shantel. If we didn't sort this out quickly, he would give up on helping them, no matter what he might get out of it. I wasn't in any position to go to Midnight and negotiate on the Shantel's behalf on my own, and I couldn't stand to just walk away—assuming I even *could* leave anymore. "The Shantel have never traded with Midnight before. Whether or not you think this is necessary, I'm sure none of you thinks it's a good idea. Maybe the forest is responding to your desires, instead of your commands. Either way, I'm sure the sakkri can control it. One of you can escort us—"

"The sakkri doesn't leave Shantel land," Shane reflexively interrupted.

"The sakkri is going to burn with the rest of us if we don't do something differently," I replied.

"If Shane travels with us, and the sakkri leads us, we can all reach the edge of Midnight's land together," Vance suggested. "Shane and the sakkri can stay behind while I go ahead to make the deal. That way, once the arrangements have been made, we don't have to worry about any of us being stuck in the forest."

"No," Shane protested vehemently. "I am not going to bring her—" He broke off, dropped his gaze, and took a deep breath. "I'll speak to my father and see if he has any other thoughts. In the morning, we will all confer to make sure we are all in agreement," he continued, looking at the older sakkri, "and then I alone will accompany you and Kadee out of Shantel land."

I knew how the Shantel felt about their sakkri, and I was not surprised that Shane would flat-out refuse to let one of them bring us out of this forest. A royal escort should prove just as effective . . . but none of this *should* have happened in the first place.

Vance and I exchanged a skeptical glance. I shrugged. It was probably the best offer we would get at this point.

"I will meet you in the Family home in the morning," Shane said as he turned to leave.

With those words, he left the two of us alone with the sakkri.

"If Shane is the one supposedly leading us out of the forest, and he decides that he does not want to sell himself into Midnight, what happens?" I asked.

"Shane is a prince dedicated to his people," the sakkri replied. "Our magic will respond to his will and his deeply set beliefs, not to his fears and whims."

"That's nicely optimistic," Vance remarked. "Kadee, where do we sleep around here? I'm exhausted."

I glanced at the sakkri, but she had already turned back to the temple, dismissing us.

"This way." Marcel had stayed out of the way during my conversations with Shane and the deathwitch, but now stepped up again to act as escort. "I am sure the Family will allow you to stay in the royal home if you wish, but we also have campsites, which are normally used by traveling merchants. I suspect children of Obsidian would be more comfortable there."

"Thank you," Vance said, looking at Marcel with curiosity.

There was a long pause, during which I wondered if I should introduce them. I ended up saying, "Vance, this is Marcel. She ..." *She kidnapped me once.* "She's our escort while we are here."

"Nice to meet you," Vance said, in a questioning tone that said he had heard the hesitation in my voice, and wasn't sure whether or not he was supposed to dislike Marcel. He started to offer his hand and then withdrew it, his eyes taking in the marks of power along Marcel's skin.

"It's a pleasure to meet another wanderer," Marcel replied. If Vance's refusal to shake her hand offended her, she did not show the emotion. "You are a long way from the home of your blood."

Vance shook his head incredulously, not deigning to comment, and Marcel led us to the merchants' campsite.

Each site had a lean-to-style tent set next to a fire ring. Heavy trunks inside each shelter held additional supplies, which were available for visitors.

I could imagine how busy this place might be when full. Now it was utterly quiet. Once Marcel bid us good night and left us on our own, Vance started to build up the fire, and I removed an extra set of blankets from the chest. It was warm enough here in the village that I didn't need any bedding beyond the soft ground, but when Vance slept in human form, he always liked to be so covered he was practically sweltering.

If he thought we were ready to sleep, though, he was mistaken. We needed to talk first. I wasn't going to let him run off alone again. I was willing to give him a little time to think, and let him bring up the subject first, but we weren't going to close our eyes until I had spoken my mind.

CHAPTER 12

WE WERE HALFWAY through dinner before I lost patience and asked, "Are we going to talk about why you stormed out of here earlier?"

"I didn't storm out. I ..." He avoided looking at me as he said, "I wouldn't have come here if I knew what the Shantel would ask of us. Maybe that makes me a coward. I don't know."

"You don't have to go," I said, though I had begun to feel obligated to the Shantel. "We can meet up with the others, and I'll go with Farrell or Malachi—" I broke off as I remembered Malachi's last trip to Midnight, when Jeshickah had locked him in a cell and held him hostage until we brought back a cure for her trainers.

"Not Malachi," Vance said before I could amend my words. "And not Farrell either."

I wondered if he was thinking about Lucas's warning: *Watch your back.* "Then we'll go—together," I said firmly.

"I saw the look in your eyes," he said. "When I asked what they were offering, you turned to me, and it was like I had just slapped you."

"You asked the questions that needed to be asked," I said. "I'm grateful for that, because I want to help the Shantel, and I know I can't do that on my own. If I looked horrified, it's because I *am,* by this situation. The Shantel can be arrogant, but they do not deserve to burn for daring to stand up to Midnight. *That* is what horrifies me—not you."

Vance still looked skeptical. "The funny thing is," he said in a tone that suggested there was nothing funny about it, "you and Lucas both act like I know what I'm doing. I knew there were slaves when I lived in Midnight, of course, but I didn't ever witness the trading. Everything I know about negotiating comes from seeing Lady Brina or Lord Daryl argue with merchants or witches about the price of painting supplies, or the spells on the greenhouse. I never thought I would apply those skills to *people.*"

I reached out, and he let me take his hand and lean against him. I could feel the heat of his body, so much warmer than any serpent, even through our clothes. His heart was pounding.

"I don't want to take you into that place," he said. "I'm doing this because . . . well, because I'm probably an idiot, but I think it's the right thing to do. It's the only option we have that doesn't involve running away like cowards from a problem we helped create. But I don't want to show you the people I used to know. The ones who knew *me*."

I let out a dismissive huff. "You don't need to *take* me anywhere. I'll go on my own—my choice."

Vance shook his head, so his long hair tickled my cheek. "Child of Obsidian," he said, with a good deal more fondness than any outsider. "You take that more seriously than most of the guild."

"I can't speak for everyone, but I learned it all from Farrell. Shkei told me about the Obsidian guild when I was still living among the serpiente, but it was like a fairy tale. Farrell made it real for me."

Vance shrugged off my attempt to credit the founder of our guild. "When you and Malachi first brought me back to the Obsidian camp, I think Farrell would have kicked me out if he had been willing to break his own edict against taking charge. He obviously didn't trust me. *You're* why I joined, and why I stayed. You made me believe we really could be free. We could make our own decisions, and didn't need to decide between ruling and being ruled. It isn't easy, but it's *good*."

It isn't easy, but it's good. That was what I needed to hold on to.

We passed a restless night. The morning felt like it dawned too early, yet when we went to the Family home, we were informed by the older sakkri and Lucas that Shane had already gone to the temple.

As we entered the temple, Shane and the younger sakkri were in the back room. Their murmuring voices reached us.

"We have had this conversation a thousand times," Shane said. "It's the only way. If Midnight—"

"Midnight doesn't have the power to burn this forest!" she protested. "We are safe here."

"We don't know that," he replied. "Even you have said you do not know what magic they may have at their disposal, and your sister says the danger is real if we continue to ignore Midnight."

"This isn't the *time*," she insisted. "There is a moment. I cannot see it clearly yet, but it will come. The players are moving into place. But if you go now, Midnight will destroy you before the white queen rises."

"We cannot delay anymore. I cannot risk everyone for—"

The sakkri's words about a white queen drew me forward like lodestone, and my shoulder brushed the dangling tendrils of a chime hanging from the ceiling, sending it dancing. At the sound, Shane stopped. He reached to hold the curtain aside, and both of their gazes fell heavily on us.

The sakkri said to Shane, "I will do what I can to ensure you travel safely. I—" She glanced at Vance and me once more before she said, "Go. All of you. Just go."

She turned her back to us until Shane grabbed my arm and Vance's and ushered us both out.

"She does not seem entirely convinced," I remarked as neutrally as I could.

The exchange also hadn't seemed like a conversation between a prince and his spiritual advisor ... but what did I really know about the royal family's connection to the sakkri? Maybe that was how they always interacted.

Somehow, I doubted it.

"The mind can be convinced by rational arguments," Shane answered. "The heart and soul are not as easy to sway. I wouldn't say my heart is entirely convinced I want to do this either."

I wanted to ask about the sakkri's reference to a "white queen," but Shane turned from us to lead the way and, I suspected, to hide the tears in his eyes. One thing had been clear: the Shantel prophet was convinced that, no matter what might happen to Midnight, this was the end for Shane. He was sacrificing himself to save his people, not to save himself.

"You two ride, correct?" Shane asked as we reached a small stable with a half dozen horses. I nodded in response to Shane's question. Vance asked, "I thought it wasn't safe to ride in the Shantel forest."

"It usually isn't," Shane answered. "We can. Our horses were bred and raised in this forest, like any Shantel woman or man."

At that point, it seemed like anything that would get us to Midnight faster would be a relief to me.

The thought made me cringe. I did not want to die with

the Shantel when Midnight took its revenge, and getting out of this forest and to Midnight seemed like the best way to save ourselves—and possibly them. But the notion of wanting to not only get to Midnight, but get there swiftly, was disturbing.

I did not know the breed of the horses that Shane saddled for us, but the prince himself brushed each one down and greeted it by name before introducing them to us. Vance responded as if meeting a dear friend, and cheerfully offered a treat to his horse, Yarrow, when Shane provided one.

When he swung up into the saddle, I saw him the way Midnight's people must have seen him: handsome, strong, and casually confident on horseback. He could have been a centaur instead of a quetzal. If he was nervous about the task at hand, he hid it well.

I regarded my own horse, Sadie, with less enthusiasm. I had learned to ride at the serpiente palace, but that had been long ago, and I hadn't much enjoyed it. This horse was a mottled gray-brown color, like the leaves that fell to the forest floor, and seemed to look at me with more intelligence than I had ever seen in an animal.

"Let's go," Vance said.

Shane led the way, and I could not help but look at the people who had gathered to bid us farewell. They lingered at the edge of the Family Courtyard, outside the stable, and on the first path we traveled. The eyes that were dry were steely and angry.

Shane did not meet anyone's gaze, but I could tell from his posture that it was a struggle not to turn back. How much of their despair was ringing in his head despite his efforts to block it out?

Only after we had left the Family Courtyard behind did I hear his breath hitch, just once.

I pulled up beside him, though I didn't know what I could possibly say that would be comforting at this point.

The day was long, interrupted by few breaks and even less conversation. As dusk fell, Shane directed us to a campsite, where he demonstrated a higher level of competence than I would have expected from a prince. Apparently even Shantel royals knew how to live in the wild.

We fed and watered the horses before sitting down. The Shantel had provided us with supplies, which Shane turned into a meal that in other circumstances probably would have been quite pleasant. If it had been shared by friends around a midsummer fire, it surely would have been accompanied by lively chatter, and maybe singing.

"How many days will it take us to get to the edge of Shantel land?" I asked. I did not ask how long it would take to get to Midnight, but the question was surely implied.

Shane paused and closed his eyes. I wondered if he had a map of the land in his head, which he could consult that way, before he said, "We should reach the edge of this land by midday tomorrow."

"Do we need to post any kind of watch, or are we safe to sleep?" Vance asked.

"We're safe," Shane answered.

So we all prepared for bed. The Shantel prince changed form and chose to sleep as a tawny-colored cougar stretched out on the bare earthen floor of the forest.

Vance pulled me aside to ask, "Do you think we should keep watch over *him*?"

I shook my head. "Maybe once we're outside of Shantel land, but there's no point here. If he decides he wants to get away from us while we're still in his land, setting a watch won't make any difference."

If Shane wanted to get away, we would turn around and find him gone. We wouldn't be able to track him, and even if Vance lifted into the air a single breath later, he wouldn't see any sign.

"Do you think the sakkri was talking about Misha?" he asked. "The white queen?"

"I don't know." I remembered what Marcel had said about how prophecy always came true, that there was no point in working toward or against it. Even if the Shantel did believe Misha would be influential in the fall of Midnight, they wouldn't do anything to help her. "I don't have the heart to ask Shane," I admitted.

Vance nodded his agreement. How did one have a conversation about hope for the future with a man who clearly didn't have any?

Chapter 13

SOMETHING WOKE ME, jerking my eyes open and tensing my muscles. I sat up, instinctively reaching for a weapon, and found Shane sitting in human form by the fire, looking at me with alarm.

"Nightmare?" he asked.

Maybe. I nodded, though the truth was, I didn't remember and was glad for that. My mind held too much material for nightmares lately.

Nearby, Vance was still sleeping peacefully. Whatever sound had disturbed me must have been in my own dreams, or he would have been awake as well.

"Did you sleep at all?" I asked Shane.

He shook his head and admitted, "I don't dare try."

I couldn't fault him for that, and what harm could missed sleep do him now? Maybe, by the time we reached Midnight, he would be too exhausted to be scared.

"Do you trust him?" he asked softly, nodding to Vance.

"What do you mean?" I asked. Of course I trusted Vance. Maybe not quite unconditionally, but I didn't trust *anyone* that much. I trusted Vance not to hurt me intentionally, or to betray our guild if he had a choice.

"Do you trust him to honor our agreement?"

"Yes." That, I could answer without hesitation. Though I added, "Unless the magic makes it impossible. He won't sacrifice us to save you, or your people, if it comes to that."

Shane nodded. "If I bring you both to Midnight's land, and wait there for Vance to make a deal, there's nothing to stop him from giving my location to them without ever negotiating for my people's safety. He could sell me to the vampires for his own profit, and leave my forest to burn."

My eyes widened. "He wouldn't do that."

"He was raised there," Shane said. "He's one of them. How do I know he didn't turn back the first time because this was his plan all along, to get me to go with you? Maybe the forest assaulted him because it knew he would betray us."

"He's one of *us*," I insisted. "Obsidian."

"The Obsidian guild lives a hard life in winter," Shane pointed out. "Who's to say this isn't an opportunity for the little quetzal to buy back his mistress's favor?"

I shook my head. I understood why Shane felt the way

he did, but he didn't know Vance. Some days even I wondered if Vance would leave the Obsidian guild, and return
to Midnight or the Azteka, but if he went he would go
alone.

"There's a reason my people don't let escaped slaves return, Kadee," Shane warned. "Even a *day* in that place can
be enough to warp someone. Vance had fourteen years."

"I was born human," I argued. "I spent years in a human
town with human parents, and then I lived in the serpiente
royal palace, with Hara Kiesha Cobriana the closest thing I
had to a sister. What does that make me? Not human, and
certainly not royalty. We are what we make ourselves, not
what others want to make us."

Shane stood, stretched, and crossed to one of the sturdy
trees that ringed this campsite. As he set a hand against
the rough bark—for support, or to talk to the tree, I didn't
know and didn't much care—I glanced at Vance and realized his eyes were open. He had probably heard everything
we said, both about him and about me.

How badly had Shane's doubts stung him? "Vance,
Shane didn't mean—"

"He did," Vance answered as he sat up. Across the
clearing, I saw Shane sigh, but he didn't look back to acknowledge our conversation. "I don't care what the Shantel
think of me. Thank you, though, for defending me."

"You're one of us," I answered. I wanted to say more, but
I didn't want Shane to know anything about the personal

fears Vance had shared with me about his return to Midnight. The Shantel prince was still near enough to overhear everything we said.

There was a pause, and I saw the thoughtful expression on Vance's face that meant he was considering how to say something. I knew what he probably thought of humans. Was he worried he would offend me if he asked about what I had said, or was he already reevaluating what he thought of me?

I went back to our conversation a few days ago, after Farrell had helped me when I had woken from my nightmare shaking.

"The first seizures came when I was a child," I said, easing into the topic but not hiding from it. "My parents . . . my *human* parents . . . didn't know what caused them or how to cure them. Marcel saw me, and understood what was happening. She took me from my parents and back to her people before the seizures could kill me." I tried to keep my voice even, but those simple words summarized so many fearful parts of my history.

I saw Shane glance back at us as if he would add something, but then he stepped off into the trees instead. I didn't chase him. As I had said to Vance before, if a prince of the Shantel wanted to disappear in this forest, he would do so. For now, I thought he was trying to give us privacy.

"How can you be a serpent if your parents were human?" Vance finally asked.

"For the same reason you aren't an Azteka priest," I answered. "My blood-father was a traveling merchant of some kind. He seduced my mother and abandoned her before he knew I existed. The man I consider my real father married my mother and raised me as his own. He didn't care that I wasn't his blood."

I was thinking of Vance's place in the Obsidian guild when I referred to his not being what his birth could have made him. When his gaze went distant, I realized he was thinking of something quite different.

Vance grabbed my hand and squeezed it once, but didn't look at me when he said, "I'm not sure you'll believe me, but I know how you feel."

I wasn't sure how to reply to that. Vance's "parents," the ones who had raised him despite his Azteka bloodlines, had been sadistic vampires. He didn't talk about them much, but that one sentence told volumes.

"I'm sorry," I said. "Vance, if you ever want to talk about them . . . that's okay."

I didn't know if I could tolerate many sentimental stories about creatures who enslaved and tortured humans and shapeshifters alike for fun and profit, but trying was the least I could do.

Apparently I wasn't the only one who didn't want to hear an answer. Shane broke unapologetically into our conversation, saying, "We should move on."

"It's still dark," I replied, startled both by the suggestion and by his presence. I had actually forgotten he was there. Shantel magic, or had my own worries about Vance's reaction just eclipsed concerns about Shane in my mind? I wanted to continue the conversation with Vance . . . but not here, not now, not with Shane nearby.

"Yet we're all awake," Shane replied. "The sun will follow soon enough."

In most places, I would have argued that traveling by horseback in the nighttime forest wasn't a good idea, but who was I to argue with a man whose mind was magically melded with these woods?

Despite the early start, we did not reach the edge of Shantel land by midday, as Shane had said we would. We trudged along, stopping only to gather water as we passed a stream and to rest the horses sometime in the early afternoon. The Shantel forest always twisted the light, making it impossible to judge direction by it, but as the sun began to sink toward the trees behind us, even I could tell we had been traveling the wrong way. The Family Courtyard should have been to the east, with Midnight to the west.

Vance flew to the tops of the trees to confirm what we all already knew: even traveling with a prince of the Shantel, we were lost in these woods.

"Well?" Vance demanded as he returned to the ground and human form. "You say you can feel the forest's edge. Where is it?"

"I don't . . ." Shane dismounted his horse and knelt on the ground, dropping his head with his fingers splayed in the dirt as if trying to beg it to let up its secrets. "It feels like we should be almost there. It has felt that way all day. I don't understand."

I had resisted asking since I saw Shane with her yesterday morning, had resisted asking while we wandered— quite possibly in useless circles—all day long, but now I needed to know.

"Are you and the sakkri lovers?"

Shane looked up with such horror on his face that he did not need to say a word.

"Oh, hell," Vance swore, turning away to lean his forehead with a thump against a nearby tree.

"It's not like that," Shane said, the age-old denial of everyone who has ever done something outrageously stupid, and been caught.

"Not like . . ." I trailed off, because there were no words strong enough to describe how pathetically useless it was for him to protest. "That's what the sakkri were fighting about," I said. "The sakkri is supposed to be untouchable, unclaimed by any mortal in any way. She—"

"Do you think I don't know that?" Shane snapped, shouting.

"Then you two are why we can't get out of this forest," Vance replied. "Your connection to each other is stronger than the rational side everyone keeps insisting should win out."

"It happened *once*," Shane hissed, "and we both knew it was wrong. It's been over for months."

"Tell that to the woman who is going to let us all die rather than let us take you to Midnight," I said.

How were we going to get out of this one? The sakkri's connection to and conscious power over the land relied on her detachment from mortal concerns. Even if we reasoned with her, there was no way of knowing if she still had enough control to override her own instincts and desires.

Vance shook his head. "You kept this information from us, when you knew damn well it was why you haven't been able to get out, and why I couldn't get out on my own. That's grounds for me to break the deal I made with your people. Kadee, do you agree it's time for us to leave?"

Did he know, when he looked at me with that cold, focused gaze, that I wanted to turn and run?

"We can't abandon them all, just because two of them made a mistake."

"Then give me another option," Vance said.

If we stayed here, and Midnight burned the forest, we would get caught in the pyre. Reasonably or not, the younger sakkri clearly believed Midnight couldn't threaten them here, so appealing to her to protect Shane wouldn't work. Even if I shared her confidence, I did not want to remain a prisoner in the Shantel woods forever.

Reluctantly, I admitted, "We can't fight Shantel magic. We shouldn't die for it."

"You made a deal with our people, and our sakkri agreed to it," Shane said. "Both of them did, even if one of them disapproved. I fear you're probably locked in the same trap as the rest of us."

"Do you think so?" Vance asked.

"Normally I can't feel outsiders in the land as well as my own people," Shane explained, "but I can feel you both. That means the land is holding on to you."

Vance shrugged. "That same land is acting to protect you, right?" Shane nodded. "And it doesn't require the conscious knowledge or response from the sakkri to make a decision?" Again, Shane nodded.

It seemed to happen in an instant. One moment Shane was kneeling on the ground and Vance was still astride his horse. The next, Vance had Shane's hair balled in his left hand and a knife at the prince's throat.

I dismounted and started toward them, but Vance glared at me warningly, while Shane went very, very still.

"I can think of a sure way to make this forest get rid of us in a hurry," Vance remarked.

"You're bluffing," Shane replied. The slight movement of his throat caused the edge of Vance's blade to draw a bead of blood to his skin. "Magic reacts to intent, not just words."

"Am I?" Vance asked. "The way I see it, it's your skin or ours."

"You're not a murderer."

"Your people made me kill over a dozen people, actually."

"Vance," I said softly, "this isn't—"

Vance's attention turned to me just for an instant, and Shane used that moment to act. He grabbed the quetzal's wrist with one hand, long enough to shove the blade away and throw himself to the side. Vance started to respond—

But Shane was gone.

We both instinctively tried to follow, and that was when I heard the order: *"Drop your weapons, or you won't draw another breath."*

CHAPTER 14

THE SHANTEL FOREST had indeed let us go, and dropped us in the middle of the serpiente royal delegation. By the time Vance and I gained our bearings, there were four guards facing us, two pointing bows and the others circling behind us with drawn swords.

It was too late to run for it. They would shoot us before we took two steps.

I had my bow, but my hands were already empty, and it seemed safer to hold them out to my sides rather than reaching for a weapon. Out of the corner of my eye, I saw Vance's knife fall to the ground. I wished I knew exactly where we were. If we were on serpiente land, we were dead. If we were on Midnight's land, we might still have a chance. Either way, I was tired of being disarmed. It wasn't like I would win in a fair fight against a trained guard anyway.

"We apologize for coming so near your camp," I said, keeping my hands carefully away from my weapons so they didn't have an excuse to shoot me. I glanced around, hoping Hara wasn't about to appear through the trees to identify me. "The Shantel forest dropped us here rather abruptly. We'll leave, if you'll let us."

The style of our clothes and weapons gave us away as Obsidian, but if we were in Midnight's land, they were supposed to let us go unless we threatened them. On the other hand, we were part of the Obsidian guild and we were probably within shouting distance of their princess. They could reasonably consider that a threat all by itself.

"Kadee." One of the guards that had moved to flank us spoke my name, and my blood ran cold. "Do you really expect us to let you disappear into the woods, so you can sneak up again behind our backs?"

Any chance I had of escaping this intact disappeared. We had to be on Midnight's land, or else they would have shot us both by now, but I was wanted for treason and had walked armed into the royal camp. According to Midnight's laws, that gave these guards freedom to do whatever they wanted with me.

I could still save Vance.

"Are you going to slaughter Vance Ehecatl on Midnight's land?" I asked, using Vance's full name, the one we almost never bothered with in the Obsidian guild. These guards would know it. It was their job to know anyone who might be a threat, either actively—like me—or because they were important. Vance, with his unspecified ties to Midnight, fell into the latter category. "We're on our way to Midnight in order to negotiate a deal on behalf of the Shantel Family," I added. "If we don't arrive, Midnight will wonder why."

The last bit was a complete fabrication, but these guards wouldn't know that. They wouldn't risk killing Vance if it might bring Midnight's wrath down upon them and their royal charge.

The guard with his bow pointed at Vance wavered slightly as he glanced at the man who was probably his commander. "Sir?" he asked. "Do we let him go?"

"Midnight only needs one to make a deal," the guard who had recognized me pointed out.

"Children of Obsidian have an irritating tendency to come back for each other," the commander replied. "Liam, go get your Arami. This isn't our decision to make."

Arami was the word the serpiente used to describe the heir to the throne, which meant the guard who responded was on his way to get Hara. Unfortunately, we still had bows pointed at us, and serpiente guards had fast reflexes. Even if they weren't certain they wanted to kill Vance, they wouldn't hesitate to shoot if we made an attempt to flee.

"We could escort them both back to Midnight," the one with a bow pointed at me suggested.

I fought the impulse to bolt in the hope that Hara

would reject that plan, but made a decision on the spot: if they decided to bring me to Midnight, I would run, and force them to kill me if I had to. If I went into that place "escorted" by royal guards, I wouldn't ever come back out.

It couldn't have been more than a minute or two, but it seemed like an interminable amount of time passed before Liam returned, not with Hara, but with Aaron—Farrell's blood-son, and Julian Cobriana's adopted son.

I almost made the mistake of stepping forward, which would have elicited an arrow in my gut. Aaron and I hadn't been close when I lived in the palace, but he hadn't been horrible to me either. I didn't think he would sell me to Midnight, anyway. A clean execution was more likely.

The commander had called him Arami. *Why?*

No, he had said, "*your* Arami." A joke, or something more serious?

I kept my mouth shut, but tucked the information away in my mind.

Aaron's eyes widened when he saw me. As he grabbed my shoulder and pulled me forward, my breath caught in sudden terror until I realized he was not attacking me, but rather hugging me.

"Sir—"

"Put up your weapons, you fools," Aaron snapped over his shoulder, glaring at the archer who had an arrow pointed at me.

"Sir," the commander began again, "it isn't safe for you to—"

"Put up your weapons and give us some space," Aaron commanded, voice hard and gray eyes flinty. He was in that moment every inch a prince, but for some inexplicable reason he had greeted me not as an outlaw, but as someone dear to him.

He has Farrell's eyes, I thought. *If only he knew.*

"Kadee," Vance asked as the guards reluctantly put away swords and bows and backed away, "are you all right?"

I nodded, though I wasn't sure he could see it. Were there tears in my eyes? Why was I crying?

"I've missed you," Aaron said softly in my ear. "You went away too quickly for me to say goodbye."

"I was guilty of treason," I reminded him.

He shrugged, releasing me partway but keeping a hand on my shoulder before he asked the one question no one had ever asked. "How many times did Hara's guard hit you before you hit him back?"

I hit Paulin with a knife, I thought, but even that wasn't the worst of it. "I let an assassin into the palace, remember?" I said bitterly. That had been the charge, anyway.

"Shkei." The name hit me like a blow when he said it. "Right? The white viper?"

Why wasn't he calling me a traitor? I struggled uselessly to form words, but none came.

"I am so sorry for what—" Aaron actually seemed to fight to suppress a sob, for someone who had to have been a stranger to him. "I do not have the authority at this time to grant you safety in serpiente land," he said, "but please believe me that when I do, I will see that the entire Obsidian guild is pardoned."

"Some of us are more guilty than others." At least there was supposed to be a trial for treason. The serpiente had other crimes that did not get trials. "Farrell Obsidian is wanted for rape." Next to that, even the accusation that he murdered Elise was nothing.

"Do you know who accused him?" Aaron asked.

I shook my head. The accusation had been made long ago, and under serpiente law, the accuser did not need to reveal him or herself publicly.

"It was my mother," Aaron said, reading my silence, and then my surprise at the words. "She told Julian that was why she left the Obsidian guild. It was how she met Julian in the first place, since the Diente deals with all accusations of high crime."

"He wouldn't—Farrell wouldn't ever—"

I didn't get through the protest because Aaron added, "It seems even less likely when you consider that they were lovers for years before then. I almost wonder if Farrell told her to lie so Julian wouldn't put her on trial for the guild's supposed crimes."

"You ... you know about them?" I asked. My gaze went to the guards, but Aaron had waved them back far enough that they were watching with scowls on their faces, but could not overhear our hushed voices. Only Vance was still near enough to overhear us, though his gaze was focused on the distant guards. If they started toward us again, Vance was ready to alert me so we could run.

"Yes, I know about my father," Aaron answered. "Misha told me."

"Mish—*when?*" I tried to imagine how Aaron and Misha could even have met, with the exception of the one time she had been brought to the palace as a criminal to be tried and executed.

"We've met regularly for months now," Aaron said, sounding puzzled. "She never mentioned it?"

I shook my head. Misha sometimes left camp for a couple of days at a time; she didn't explain her movements, and I had always assumed she just needed some time by herself. Misha had obviously spent part of those meetings arguing our case with Aaron—quite successfully—but I couldn't help but be suspicious. Why all the secrecy? "Where do you meet?"

"The palace, usually," Aaron answered. "I've offered to meet her somewhere else—I know how dangerous it is for her to come there—but nothing frightens her." He said the last words with a grin that reflected pride and admiration.

Misha had done more than just tell Aaron about his heritage. The expression on his face when he described her was that of a man who was more than just smitten.

Aaron had always been nice enough to me, but I had never expected this level of acceptance from him. Diente Julian might not have been his father by blood, but the cobra had raised Aaron as his own son, and Aaron had never had a chance to know his mother, who had died in childbirth. Now he was acting as if he was one of us, not one of them.

Irrationally, I found myself wanting to shake him. I bit back my arguments because having Aaron on our side helped us, but I wanted to demand, *A few weeks with Misha, a few months at most, and you're willing to betray the man who raised you?* I knew why I loved the Obsidian guild, but Aaron had no reason to turn his back on the only family he had ever known for relative strangers. Did he even understand how enormous a decision he was making, or was this just another prince's whim? Did he think he could just say he *wanted* both the throne and the freedom of the Obsidian guild, and the universe would mercifully bend to his whims? The world wasn't that easy.

"Don't get yourself arrested either," I said, more in response to my own thoughts than to the conversation we had been having. "You have a good life."

"I'm not going to get arrested," Aaron replied. "I intend to take the throne."

"You're the younger child, and though I wish it didn't

matter, you're a boa, not a cobra," I pointed out, though I couldn't forget the words I had heard: *your Arami.* At least one guard here supported him. If he took the throne, and then took Misha as his mate . . .

Impossible.

"I am the child of Diente Julian Cobriana, blood or not. He has made that clear." The irony in his voice was evident. "More importantly, I am the only one in the royal family who is willing to refuse to violate everything the serpiente stand for in order to keep Midnight happy."

"In that case, what are you doing here?" Vance asked, speaking up for the first time. "Were you with Hara's group in the market?"

I hadn't seen him, but Midnight's market was a vast and chaotic place.

"Hara met with Midnight's bailiffs to balance our accounts," Aaron said. "I cut across the market to see what rumors I could gather from the other merchants. We met up afterward, but Hara turned back when the Shantel forest rejected her," he explained. "I wanted to keep trying. Given some of the rumors we've heard, I thought the forest might react differently to me than it did to her."

I knew why the forest had rejected Hara and would reject Aaron, but I still asked, "Rumors?" What information had made it to the serpiente, either from Midnight or from the Shantel?

Aaron hesitated, as if for the first time realizing to

whom he was speaking. "You told my guards you're on your way to Midnight," he said. "Why?"

Unless I decided to trust him, we were at an impasse. Without going into detail, I explained, "The Shantel asked us to negotiate for them."

That was consistent with what we had told the guards, so it didn't lose us the tenuous protection we had based on Midnight's laws, but it didn't necessarily mean we were working *for* Midnight.

Aaron still didn't seem convinced, which was fine. I didn't need to know everything, as long as he stayed friendly enough that he let us go. After a long pause, and an assessing glance at Vance—the first time he had acknowledged the quetzal at all—he sighed, shook his head, and explained.

"Rumors say the Shantel tried to fight Midnight somehow, and have now locked Midnight out of their forest, either to protect themselves from retaliation or perhaps even in blatant rebellion. I thought the forest might let me in because I'm willing to support them."

My skin crawled, hearing him say words like that. *Here.* In Midnight's forest. In front of two people known to have dealings with the vampires. What had we said or done to make him trust us this way? He shouldn't.

At the same time, I couldn't help thinking, *No wonder Midnight is demanding flesh, if there are rumors like that. Shane will be their proof that the Shantel are still fully under Jeshickah's control.*

Aaron continued. "Julian still sells our criminals to Midnight," he said. "He willingly pays Midnight's tariffs, and allows Midnight's mercenaries into our land, and then has the nerve to try to denounce that empire as if he doesn't support it every day. His daughter will follow his policies. I won't."

"The speech is nice," Vance said, "but how do you intend to keep Midnight from destroying you as soon as you raise a hand against them?"

"If we can get support from the Shantel, with their magic—"

Aaron broke off when I shook my head. "The Shantel are trapped in their own land," I admitted. "Their attempt against Midnight failed, and Midnight has demanded payment. The forest won't let you in because the Shantel don't trust anyone else not to turn them in for the bounty."

"We're going to Midnight now to try to explain the situation, and buy the Shantel more time before the vampires try to burn them out," Vance added.

Are we still? I wondered, but didn't challenge him aloud, since I had been telling the serpiente we were on our way to Midnight, too.

Aaron nodded slowly. After his speech against Midnight, I wondered what he thought of our current intentions.

"Do what you need to do," he said. "I will bring word back to the serpiente about the Shantel. Maybe we can find some way to help." I doubted it, but I nodded anyway. Aaron hugged me again, saying, "Be careful, Kadee. Hopefully, I will see you soon."

He returned to his guards and snapped an order about letting us go peacefully, which left me feeling dazed. Vance picked his knife back up and we moved away swiftly, not wanting to test our luck.

"That was ... unexpected," Vance said, the words a gross understatement.

Aaron's bizarre behavior had to be the frustrated result of high hopes, few prospects, and new love—though I had a hard time imagining Misha, as angry and bitter as she had been since her return from Midnight, engaged in such giddy infatuation.

Even before it came time to rise up against Midnight, I did not see how Aaron could follow through with anything he had said. Hara Kiesha Cobriana was a royal cobra and first in line to the throne. Not all serpiente loved her, but they all respected her and what a cobra form stood for, too much so for Aaron to easily stage a coup.

On the other hand, were we any different, believing in Malachi's prophecy? Our dreams seemed just as impossible, yet what I had seen from Aaron today made it clear they were closer than ever.

There is a moment. I cannot see it clearly yet, but it will come. The players are moving into place. But if you go now, Midnight will destroy you before the white queen rises.

Had that been prophecy Vance and I overheard in the sakkri's tent? If so, did it mean that even the sakkri—who was marked by the land at birth, and whose prophecies the Shantel treated as immutable fact—believed the end was in sight? Not soon enough to save Shane, but . . .

The white queen rises.

CHAPTER 15

"DO YOU WANT to talk?" Vance asked, once we had put a little space between us and the serpiente royal party.

I shook my head. If Aaron succeeded and somehow took the throne, we would hear, and if he got arrested for treason, we would hear that, too. If he ended up needing to flee the palace, he would be able to find us. Malachi's spells wouldn't keep Farrell's son away, especially since he was apparently close to Misha as well.

"Are we still going to Midnight?" I asked.

"Do you think we should?"

"It's probably the last thing I *want* to do," I answered, "but I feel like we owe it to them. I'm not sure how seriously Midnight will take us when we need to admit that the Shantel may have trouble delivering payment, but maybe we can learn something useful, like whether Midnight really has the power to burn the forest. Maybe the sakkri is right, and they're bluffing. The sakkri seems to believe there's hope if they just hold out a little longer."

"Or maybe we can find proof that Midnight has the power to make good on their threat, and we can convince the sakkri to let Shane go." Vance's suggestion was the more cynical but likely option. "Either way, we should be very certain of our plan if we decide to go back to Shantel land. I don't want Midnight to burn down the Shantel forest if we can stop it, but I don't want to get trapped there again either."

"We'll see what Midnight says, then make our next plan," I said.

The sun was sinking, turning the sky crimson and gold ahead of us, but we decided to keep traveling until we reached our destination. Midnight's roads were well maintained, and the only predators to stalk them were the vampires themselves.

"There's no point in reaching Midnight in the morning anyway," Vance said. "We would only end up waiting for the trainers to wake."

We reached the building referred to as Midnight proper under the light of a half-moon. I had been there only once before, when we had tried to kill the trainers ... though thank God Jeshickah had never realized we were complicit in that failed plot.

That time, I had been too focused on my own terror to

really see anything we passed. This time, as we approached the massive black iron fence, I instinctively looked around for guards. The gate, though ominous, stood open. The plants around its base and the moss across the path made it clear that it was never shut.

"Where are the guards?" I asked.

Ahead of us, a white slate path lit by gently swaying lamps led through a beautiful garden before it reached the grand front doors of Midnight proper. The trees inside were bowed, their branches gracefully weeping, and the leaves that were just beginning to escape their buds were deep red. I recognized the bare, thorny branches of long-stemmed roses that had not yet put out greenery for the spring, but there were other plants I did not know. Night moths danced around blooms the color of bone-deep bruises, and I saw a fox drinking from a stone birdbath depicting a sleeping leopard.

"There are guards," Vance answered. "You don't see them, but they see us. If we looked like a threat, they would report to their masters before we ever saw them. If they didn't know me, they would intercept us once we passed the gate to ask our business." He started forward and I followed, against my better judgment. "But they do know me, so they won't give us any trouble. Look."

He paused to point to a tiny brown sparrow sitting in the gracefully draped branches of a pussy willow. In response to Vance's acknowledgement, the little bird spread its wings and ducked its head as if in a curtsy—not a natural position for a bird.

"Shapeshifter?" I asked.

I had expected vampire guards. Even knowing that the market guards were all shapeshifters, I hadn't thought that they would be trusted to do that kind of work here in the heart of the empire.

Vance nodded. "Most of the guards are."

I couldn't help but wonder what had driven this little sparrow to leave her own kind and come here. Was she lonely? Or did bloodtraitors like her have their own community somewhere, friends and maybe even families? Had she come here willingly, or been forced to it?

If the Obsidian guild hadn't taken me in, would I have ended up here, too?

The sparrow watched us as we approached the heavy mahogany front door. It seemed so odd that Vance could reach out, lift the latch, and let himself in as if it were nothing.

The front hall was lit with a chandelier in a vaulted ceiling, and then a series of wall sconces in the hallways leading off to the left and right. Here, both doors were blocked by posted guards in crisp uniforms. I was sure one of them was a serpent, though I didn't otherwise recognize his face.

I was still looking at the guards when Vance said, "The artwork is mostly done by members of Katama's line. That's one of Brina's paintings, there."

We were surrounded by spectacular art. Even the wooden chair rails that divided the lower section of the wall from the upper had been carved and stained to show an elaborate jungle scene. The painting that Vance had pointed out portrayed a beautiful woman with fair skin and dark hair—Mistress Jeshickah, lounging against a leopard with a white pelt, blue eyes, and black spots.

How could creatures apparently immune to the pain of those they ruled care enough to want, much less create, such breathtaking beauty?

"This way," Vance said. The serpent guard stepped aside to let us pass into a hallway just as grand as the entry. If Vance was nervous to be here, he was hiding it well.

"Why is it all so *pretty*?" I asked, disgusted by the contrast between what I saw and what I knew happened here.

"If we had gone down the other hall, you would have seen a black door, and then an end to all pretense, since that's where the common slaves sleep and do their daily work," Vance answered. "This is the wing where the trainers and most respected guests reside. If luxury didn't appeal to them, they wouldn't make such an effort to rule."

"Do we need an appointment?" I asked as we turned a corner and entered a hall lined with closed doors. This didn't seem like a place visitors were welcome.

"If we wanted to speak to Mistress Jeshickah personally, we would need an appointment," Vance answered, "but one of the trainers is probably available."

"And you know where they are, and can just knock on the door."

Whatever my voice held—terror, judgment, shame, reluctance?—it was enough to make Vance stop in his tracks and turn to me. "Yes, I can," he answered, looking uneasy. "And I will, because I want to get this over with as much as you do."

As we walked down the hallway, a woman approached us. She was petite, and stepped softly, her bare feet making no sound on the plush carpet. The dress she wore was simple, with ties at the throat and around the waist giving it much of its shape, but what caught my eye was the thin black band around her neck.

The collar was perhaps half an inch wide, and closed with a buckle that anyone could reach up to remove.

The only thing more disconcerting than the ink-black mark of ownership was the way she dropped her gaze and gave a half curtsy when she noticed Vance.

Vance hesitated, and he looked back at me with clear discomfort before he asked her, "Is Jaguar in?"

"I'm sorry, sir. I believe Master Jaguar is occupied with his new project," the woman replied, her voice soft and her gaze never rising from the floor. "He gave instructions that he was not to be disturbed this evening."

"Sir?" I echoed. It was hard to imagine anyone addressing Vance in such a way, but here was proof right in front of me.

"What about Taro?" Vance asked, ignoring me.

The woman shook her head. "He and Master Varick are in a conference with—"

"Never mind," Vance interrupted. "Kadee, we might need to wait a while after all. I'm sorry."

"I believe Master Gabriel is in, if you need to speak to one of the trainers," the woman suggested.

Vance shook his head, and told her, "You can go."

"I don't want to stay here any longer than necessary," I said. "Is Gabriel actually worse than any of the others?"

I understood why Vance didn't want to face Gabriel so soon after learning about Alasdair. I didn't want to look him in the eye either, but that didn't mean the others would actually be any kinder or easier to deal with.

The decision was made for us as one of the doors burst open, making us jump as it slammed into the wall and nearly bounced back into its frame. I thought at first that the slave we had just spoken to had fallen, but then I realized that she had gone swiftly to her knees.

The first person to emerge, however, was not a vampire.

"*Damn* you to Hell and back!" Misha spat as she stumbled into the hallway.

No! I wanted to scream. The serpiente must have captured her again, somehow, or else she single-handedly decided to assault Midnight. Misha's fair skin was darkened with bruises and raised with welts.

The man who came to the door did not seem concerned

with Misha's anger. Instead, he looked amused, especially as he glanced past her and noticed Vance and me in the hallway.

Misha turned to fix her moss-green eyes on me with a look that should have been hot enough to spark. Rage, hatred . . . madness?

"What is she doing here?" Vance demanded, insanely, of the trainer.

"Vance, it's a pleasure to see you again," the vampire replied, "but you know perfectly well I won't discuss another's private business."

People had told me many times that the trainers were handsome, and terribly charming when they wanted to be. I didn't think this one was trying to be charming, exactly, but it would have been hard to imagine him as evil if I didn't know that some of the most beautiful serpents were also often the most poisonous.

"She's not . . ." I only made it halfway through the question, because having the trainer look directly at me made my stomach twist.

"She's free to go," he answered. "Misha, it looks like I have another appointment waiting, so we'll have to continue this conversation another time."

Misha drew a deep breath and asked in a carefully even tone, "But we have our deal, right?"

"As agreed," he answered.

"That's all that matters."

She turned on her heel, but before she could leave, I posed Vance's question again. "What are you *doing* here?"

"I could ask you the same thing," she snapped back. "We're camped just a few hours to the south. I'll see you there when your *business* here is done."

She said *business* like it was something dirty. Since that was exactly how I felt about this whole situation with the Shantel, the word cut deep, silencing me while Misha stormed past us without further question or explanation.

The trainer continued our conversation as if my brief exchange with Misha had been irrelevant. "Vance, please do introduce me to your friend," he said.

"This is Kadee Obsidian," Vance answered. "Kadee, this is—" He stopped there.

The vampire chuckled, and offered his hand to me. "Gabriel," he introduced himself, though I had already guessed as much. He glanced at Vance as he said, "They say children of Obsidian don't use titles, but old habits die hard, don't they?"

Vance nodded tightly. When guards in the market talked about the vampires, they always used titles: *Mistress* or *Master* for Jeshickah and her trainers, and *Sir*, *Lord*, or *Lady* for the others. It wasn't a leap to imagine that Vance had been taught the same way.

I didn't have the nerve to refuse to shake the vampire's hand, though I wanted to. Gabriel was the one who had hired us to capture Alasdair. He was surely the one who still caused the night terrors that brought shrieks to Misha's throat in the middle of the night. And in the end, he was the one in whose not-so-tender "care" Shkei had died.

I wanted his hand to be cold and clammy, confirmation of his monstrous nature, but instead was surprised to discover that his skin was almost as warm as Vance's. People said vampires were dead, pretty corpses preserved and animated by magic, but if so, why were they warm? Why weren't they as cold as dead flesh should be?

"Is Misha all right?" I asked. He had already refused to tell Vance what Misha was doing here, so I didn't ask about that. I wanted confirmation that she hadn't been sold back in to Midnight. Was "free to go" temporary?

"Your would-be future queen is fine," Gabriel replied. "She came here of her own free will and is leaving the same way, albeit with a few more bruises, but that's the cost of asking favors sometimes. Now, what did you need?"

Not a favor, I hope.

"We've come to relay a message from the Shantel," Vance said, "and possibly to propose a deal on their behalf. Do you have time?"

"I always have time to make deals with your guild," Gabriel replied. "You do offer the prettiest toys. Vance, did you ever meet my Ashley?"

Vance nodded as the once princess of the avians came to the door.

She was as lovely as I remembered her, with creamy fair

skin and hair and eyes the color of beaten gold. The gown she wore was elegant, deep crimson velvet that flattered her form without being lewd. It was still obscene, though, because it perfectly matched the leather collar around her throat. If she recognized me as one of the ones responsible for her capture, she made no indication.

She was named after the first queen of the avians, I thought. Malachi had told me that one day, while we were stalking her, waiting for our opportunity. *You had to take even that away from her, didn't you?*

"Beautiful, fetch our guests some refreshments, and let Jeshickah know that they've come to negotiate for the Shantel," Gabriel commanded the hawk. *His slave.* "We'll meet in the library. Vance, I believe you know the way? I'll join you as soon as I have cleaned up." He held up a hand, and I realized for the first time that there was blood streaked across the back of it. His black clothing was probably hiding more. Was it all Misha's?

Whose did I want it to be?

CHAPTER 16

THE LIBRARY HAD a large conference table, and then more books than I had ever imagined. Were they history, philosophy, or just stories intended to help idle away the eternal hours? What did immortal creatures read?

I walked along the shelves and found it hard not to touch the leather-bound tomes, though Vance seemed not to care.

I couldn't remember my father's voice or face anymore, but I knew we used to read together from the Bible, as well as copies of the Declaration of Independence, which my father had considered the most beautiful writing ever created by human beings. Ever since the first seizures, letters swam in my vision. I could remember some of the words I had learned at my father's knee but would never be able to recognize them on a page now.

"How much trouble are we in?" I asked Vance, trying to pull myself away from the allure of the smooth pages. "I know we're supposed to be freeblood, and you're supposed to be welcome here, but . . . Misha is freeblood, and even I could tell the trainer was going for blood when he spoke to you."

"We are in . . ." Vance trailed off. "I have no idea how much trouble we are in. I wish I could tell you that anything they say is a lie, but that's not true. In fact, I'm not sure how often they actually lie outright. It's one of the most frightening things about them."

The door behind us opened and a tall, broad-shouldered vampire entered. Jaguar. I had never met this trainer before, but I recognized him from stories I had heard. His black hair was bound back, but it was still visibly longer than mine, and his features spoke of his heritage among both Europeans and the Azteka.

He ignored me at first, but greeted Vance with a smile and an outstretched hand. "Vance, welcome home."

Vance flinched as he shook Jaguar's hand. "It's not home anymore," he replied.

Jaguar appeared skeptical but did not press the issue. The obvious dismissal was perhaps more of a challenge than any words could be.

"You've come to us to make a deal, I hear?"

"I thought you were busy," I said, hoping to interrupt Jaguar's focus on Vance. "A new . . . project." I had a feeling

I knew what that meant for him, which was why I almost couldn't get the word out.

Jaguar confirmed my suspicions immediately, saying, "Hardly a project worth mentioning, it turns out. I'll have an empty cell again in days." He spoke as if he were talking about an animal, not a man or woman.

"We're waiting for Gabriel and . . . Jeshickah," Vance asserted, cutting in. I could tell it took a conscious effort to say the Mistress of Midnight's name without a title. The slip made Jaguar laugh.

"Work on that one," Jaguar suggested, still smiling. "But not today, while you stand in her library. She's more apt to deal when a man shows respect. Kadee, would you like a tour while Vance deals with the gritty details of trading flesh? I have no patience for such negotiations myself."

"No," Vance replied, while I was still wondering how Jaguar knew my name. "She'll stay with me."

"You'd rather keep her in a room with Jeshickah, Gabriel, Taro, and Nathaniel as you discuss someone's price than let me show her around the building?"

Taro was another trainer, and the closest thing to a father that Vance had ever had. Nathaniel was one of Midnight's mercenaries. It made sense that they would all be present, but I couldn't help but feel that this was a lot of show for little old us.

"I'd like to stay, thanks," I replied. It was a lie, and surely everyone in the room knew it. I didn't want to be alone with any of these creatures, but I refused to leave Vance alone with them either.

"It's decided, then," Vance said.

"Your choice," Jaguar confirmed as he sat, propping his feet up on a second chair.

It wasn't long before the others joined us.

Taro was a tall, slender man with nutmeg-colored skin and blond hair, which he wore long and pulled back. When he walked in, he greeted Vance with a smile and ruffled his hair affectionately. Vance tensed at the gesture as if it were a slap.

I was sure Taro *noticed;* he was a trainer, after all. The question was whether he had predicted that Vance would react that way, and chose to do it anyway, or if he had forgotten that Vance wasn't the same trusting, dependent child he had raised until recently.

When Taro turned away to confer with Jaguar in quiet tones, I caught Vance staring longingly at him for just a moment before he dropped his gaze and carefully composed himself.

Gabriel joined us next, cleaned of blood and impeccably dressed once more. "Ashley" trailed after him, carrying a tray that included sweet biscuits and tea, as if we were all here for an afternoon social.

While I had wondered about Taro's motives, I had no doubt about Gabriel's when he said to her, "Thank you, beautiful. Scribe the meeting for us, would you?"

She nodded, and replied too softly for me to hear. He had phrased it as a request, but it obviously wasn't, and she returned with writing tools before the next vampire entered the room.

Nathaniel was the one who had bought Misha and Shkei from Julian Cobriana last year before they would have been executed. I wasn't sure if I hated him or was grateful to him for that.

It was irrelevant. Even I knew you shouldn't show either of those emotions to a mercenary.

Unsurprisingly, Jeshickah joined us last.

The last time I had seen her, she had been worn, pale, tired, and angry as she dealt with the plague that had already killed a score of humans and rendered all the other trainers unconscious. Now, fully recovered, she was stunning.

She seemed to be dressed for horseback, in clothes that blended female sensuality and fashion with men's practicality—breeches and boots under a snug, emerald-green riding coat that momentarily threw me back ten years, because it was a *human* fashion, and would have been normal in a human town if it had been matched with a proper skirt and shirt.

I knew that vampires often appeared more human—more *normal*—than serpiente and other shapeshifters, but I couldn't help expecting them to look bizarre and frightening. Instead, the sight of all these individuals together made the eye want to linger, even while every instinct said to run. I did not doubt that Jeshickah had picked her trainers for their talents, but I was also sure she applied the same critical gaze to their looks as well.

When Jeshickah entered, Ashley went to her knees. Jeshickah's gaze fell on Vance, and I saw the tension thrum through him and I wondered how they had taught him these habits that he was physically fighting not to obey. Had they beaten him, in this place? If they had, how could he possibly long to return to it? I wanted to reach for him, or say something, *anything* comforting, but didn't dare.

"The prodigal son returns," Jeshickah said. Was that a slight smile on her face? It was hard to read her expression when I was afraid to meet her gaze. "And he brings a friend. Kadee Obsidian, I see you're following the path of your masters as well. How is my Farrell these days?"

Was there any acceptable way to answer that question? I didn't owe these creatures any explanation for my behavior. But I was sure she knew that, just as she knew that Farrell Obsidian may have started our guild, and been accepted as its leader, but that didn't mean he owned or ruled those within it.

"I don't know," I replied, trying to keep my voice neutral. "We haven't seen him since we left to speak to the Shantel. Do you want to deal, or play games?"

"They'll do both if you let them," Nathaniel said drily.

"Trainers can't help playing any more than a spider can resist running toward a tapped string."

Jeshickah gestured, and a young man who had been standing as silent as a shadow in the back of the room appeared and poured the tea. The others ignored him, but I couldn't resist watching as he first prepared Jeshickah's tea with honey and cream, and then poured cups for Taro and Gabriel before looking to me and Vance questioningly. He was probably close to my age. His fair skin made me wonder if he had ever seen the sun.

"Tea, Kadee?" Taro prompted softly, as if I had been asked once before.

I was cold and the honey looked good. Was that kind of reasoning the path to damnation? I nodded, and the nameless slave stepped forward to make the wordless desire a reality.

Vance declined tea, and then Jeshickah commanded, "Tell us everything you saw among the Shantel."

Over the next hour or so, I discovered that a few phrases have an intrinsically terrifying connotation when spoken in the right tone by a trainer. They were, in no particular order:

"Oh, really?"

"I see."

And, of course, "I believe that *you* believe that."

The last one was particularly unsettling. It came after

my assertion that I had been partially raised by the Shantel, and I was confident that they were telling the truth when they said that the Shantel were trying to respond to Midnight's demands, but their magic was interfering.

I believe that you believe that. In other words, Jeshickah didn't think I was lying—for which I was grateful, since getting caught lying to these people would be a very bad idea—but still thought the Shantel might be.

Since I had wondered about that myself, it was a struggle not to squirm.

Vance and I described the argument among the royal house, and even that the serpiente royal party had also been turned back from Shantel land. Without needing to discuss it, we did not share the fact that the sakkri and the prince were having an affair, or the conversation we had with Aaron. Vance detailed his experience when he first tried to leave on his own, and then how he had tricked Shane and the forest in order to get it to release us.

"You bluffed an immortal, ancient power capable of defying even natural laws of space and time?" Nathaniel paraphrased.

"It responds to the royal house," Vance replied. "If the prince can be fooled, then it can be, too."

"I see." Which, in that context, obviously meant, *You're lying. I know it. Do you know it?*

Was Vance lying? Would he have gone through with his threat if the forest hadn't released us?

Defensively, Vance added, "I owe more loyalty to Kadee than I do to the Shantel royal house."

"Naturally," Jaguar replied, studying me in a way that made my skin crawl. I had a feeling that Vance had just handed them a weapon, and it was me.

"To summarize," Jeshickah said, "the Shantel propose to offer one younger prince, with no expectations and no magical training, as full compensation for their treason."

Why did she look at me when she said that, and not Vance? Did I appear the weaker one in our pair?

Probably. I tried to gather my wits, though. "Shane does have some magical ability." I was thinking of his empathy, though how that could benefit Midnight, I had no idea.

"Oh?" Jeshickah leaned back in her chair, showing polite attention but little interest. "It must be something spectacular if they think it is sufficient to buy their safety— especially since I am not yet convinced they even plan to follow through on this deal. What incentive do I have at this point to let them barter and whine at me? I gave them an opportunity to protect the freeblood status of their people, and they refused. At the moment, I am inclined to simply burn the forest, and take for my own anyone who makes it out alive."

My whole body went cold at the thought. Could she *do* that?

Magically, I wasn't sure. Legally . . .

I rallied once more, recalling what Shane had said to me

about why Midnight had never forced them to trade in flesh before. "If you do that," I said, "you will lose all power you have over them." My voice shook a little, but I forced myself to continue. "If you declare that every Shantel's life is forfeit, and there is no way to barter or seek forgiveness, they will know the only way to protect themselves is to destroy you. You saw what one deathwitch was able to do. Do you want to force every Shantel who flees a burning forest to become a potential assassin? Or do you want an opportunity to make a profit?"

For a moment, as my heart pounded, I was proud of myself for standing up to the vampires. Then Jeshickah spoke.

"They would not be the first nation we have brought low," she said, "and whose witches still attempt to needle us. Even Vance here has fought such a creature once, gallantly defending his mistress." Her voice seemed to slice through me. I braced myself, certain the next words were going to be worse. "*If* we accept a deal with the Shantel, it will not be out of fear of retaliation, I promise you that."

She paused, took a sip of her tea, then continued. Her gaze flickered from me to Vance as she said, "What we need to establish now is not how far I am willing to go, but how far *you* are. The Shantel offered you a deal, but you are right that their actions violated its terms. You owe them nothing. What is your intention moving forward?"

The last hour had been hell, but now I realized the hard part was just beginning. Jeshickah had suggested that she might be willing to make a deal, but that meant she expected us to propose one. If Shane wasn't sufficient, what were we willing to promise on the Shantels' behalf?

As if it were the reason for my hesitation, Jeshickah added, "We would offer you compensation for your work, of course."

"We don't need anything from you," I said, but I felt less certain now. I wanted to help the Shantel, but that didn't mean I planned to work for Midnight.

Most importantly, I needed to get away from these five vampires and their perfectly black eyes, masking souls just as dark. Get away from the gentle scratching of a quill pen as the enslaved hawk diligently recorded everything we said. Get away from the scent of tea and honey, served by a young man who had probably lived his entire life in slavery.

Anxiety and exhaustion were pushing at me. My fingertips gave warning twitches. I clasped my hands together in my lap, but if I didn't have a chance to calm myself soon, those little spasms would grow to encompass my whole body.

"If we have nothing to offer you, Kadee, then you may leave," Jeshickah said. "We will continue to negotiate with our Vance."

Vance's eyes narrowed a bit at the word "our," but he said only, "I'm not sure Kadee is safe wandering this building alone."

Had he noticed my state? Had *they*? I didn't want to

leave him alone, but it seemed safer to risk walking out of the room long enough to compose myself than falling into a fit that could leave Vance forced to care for me.

"We're all here," Jaguar remarked. "Who do you think will accost her?"

"I don't know, and I don't want to learn through experience," Vance replied.

"I can escort her."

The soft, musical voice made us all turn toward the hawk in the corner.

I frowned. I had not heard anyone give her a command, though Ashley—once Alasdair—was obviously considered a broken slave, and broken slaves as a rule did not speak up without a master's order.

"That would be fine," I said. Ashley's collar clearly marked her as Gabriel's property, so no one in this building would dare assault her or someone with her except him—and as Jaguar had pointed out, the trainers were all here. In addition to needing to get out for a moment, I wanted to know why a broken slave had spoken, of what seemed to be her own free will.

Maybe she wanted to accuse me of kidnapping her and selling her into this miserable existence. If she did, it would be no worse than I deserved. I would almost welcome abuse from her, if it could help me dig my way out of the guilt I felt whenever I thought about her.

Jeshickah nodded to give permission, and without another command spoken, Ashley handed her pen to one of the other slaves and moved to guide me toward the door.

"Are you sure, Kadee?" Vance asked as I stood. He was asking *Are you all right?* but I couldn't answer that question directly.

"You make the deal you need to make," I said. "Take care of yourself and our guild, and I'll see you when you're done."

Vance did not appear convinced, but he looked at me and then around at the trainers and said, "Okay. I'll do my best here. Let me—" I had a sense that he had been about to say, "Let me know what she has to say." He was as curious about Ashley as I was.

I took my leave of the vampires gratefully, and followed Ashley from the room.

CHAPTER 17

MY THROAT FELT tight, and a fine shiver kept running up and down my spine. Before I could learn anything from the hawk, I needed to get my body under control.

"Would it be possible for us to get some fresh air?" I asked, before realizing that I didn't know if a slave was allowed outside.

"If you wish," Ashley answered before leading the way back to the front doors.

The hawk was beautiful, and seemed so serene. Could it be that there wasn't anything she was supposed to say? Was she just trying to set an example for us, so we could see both what Midnight was capable of doing to a freewilled individual . . . and how much easier it was to submit, and just let it happen?

We reached the front garden, and I was finally able to

take a deep breath of the cool night air. A fine drizzle had started to fall, but I didn't mind, and my golden-haired guide didn't say a word. As I waited for my trembling to subside, and for Ashley to share whatever was on her mind, I considered a thousand possible things I could say.

"Do you know who I am?" I finally asked.

"Kadee Obsidian," she answered promptly, still without malice in her voice. "Companion of Lord Vance, I believe."

I wasn't sure what she thought that word "companion" implied, but whether or not she correctly understood my relationship with Vance wasn't something that concerned me.

"Do you know how you got here?" I asked. She had called me Obsidian. Even if she hadn't recognized my face specifically from the kidnapping, she had to recognize that name, unless something in the process that broke her as a slave also erased those memories.

Her serene expression cracked for just an instant, to reveal what seemed like fear, but then the calm returned before she said, "I am aware that your guild facilitated the exchange."

"Fancy terms for saying we sold you into slavery."

"You had no choice."

At the time, I had told myself the exact same thing. Now, looking at this woman who had been stripped even of her name, I could only say, "Yes, we did."

She looked me in the eye, gaze direct and voice unwavering, when she said, "A trainer only offers a choice when there is no choice. The decision you had to make was between a stranger, or one of your own. What you need—" She swallowed, dropping her gaze to say, "What you need to know is that the woman you brought back may be a stranger, too. Do not trust her."

"Do you know something I need to know?" I asked. Ashley must have seen whatever transpired between Misha and Gabriel earlier that night. Had Misha betrayed us?

"I'm sure it isn't my place to decide that," she murmured in reply.

I glanced up, wondering if her sudden vagueness was related to the shapeshifter guards nearby. Could they hear our soft voices from where they were perched in bird form on the iron fence? Possibly, and we were just as likely to be overheard by guards or vampires inside.

"Did someone tell you to warn me?" If she had made the decision on her own, I needed to reevaluate my understanding of what it meant to be broken. If someone had ordered her to speak to me, that opened up worlds of possibility. Did we have an ally inside Midnight? More likely, someone had decided to unnerve us with this vague warning.

Or they wanted to split us up. I had been so desperate to leave, and so intrigued by Ashley speaking seemingly of her own accord, that I had jumped to accept her offer. It occurred to me now that Gabriel could have set up some kind of signal he could give to his slave if he saw an opportunity to separate Vance and me.

"If I've offended you, I apologize," Ashley said, though whether she was responding to my question or my expression as I realized this could have been a setup, I wasn't sure. Either way, I had a feeling I wasn't going to get an answer.

"I should get back," I said.

"As you wish."

My stomach tied up in knots, I hurried back toward the library with Ashley trailing behind me. I wasn't enough of a coward to sit on the front steps of Midnight and wait for Vance to join me, now that I had my body under control. By the time I reached the room where I had left them all, however, Jaguar was just saying good evening to Vance.

Gabriel was waiting to greet Ashley, and wrapped his arm around her waist, planting a kiss on her forehead. I was reminded of what the deathwitch had said: *he is broken, and does not know how to love something and let it be free.* If that was what love meant to a trainer, I never wanted to see hatred.

"Show these two to a guest room they can use, beautiful, then come back to me," he ordered her.

She nodded, the motion extending to her whole body, so it was almost a curtsy. Gabriel left without another word to us, and Ashley simply said, "This way."

"What's going on?" I asked Vance as we followed the hawk down the hall.

Vance shook his head, frustrated. "They are willing to

negotiate, but it isn't going to be pretty. I shared Shane's argument for why he should make a suitable payment, and pointed out that they already have Amber. Unsurprisingly, they don't think it's sufficient. Mistress Jeshickah wants to 'consider the options' and get back to us tomorrow night."

"Tomorrow night?" I hissed.

"I didn't agree," Vance said quickly. "If we stay, we can hear and discuss their offer. If you want to go, I'll go with you."

I want to go! Of course I did. I wanted to walk away and never look back. I didn't want to remain here among trainers, or listen to them say that Shane wasn't valuable enough. I didn't want to look at Ashley, and wonder if Shane would have that same doll-like poise once Midnight stripped him of everything that made him a free-willed individual. I wanted to go home to the Obsidian guild campsite.

What will you tell Farrell when he asks what you learned from the Shantel?

I would tell him they asked for our help, but that it wasn't our responsibility to save the Shantel. I could picture Farrell nodding, and telling me that I was a free individual who owed the Shantel no allegiance . . . even though they once saved my life, and were the only ones who had ever dared to try to fight Midnight, the very empire we were trying to destroy. He wouldn't say that last bit aloud, but I would see it on his face. Hadn't we become slave-traders, and sold Alasdair for Misha, partly to fulfill a prophecy that said Midnight would fall? Was I so much of a coward that I would refuse to help the Shantel because their attempt to make a difference in our warped world had brought repercussions?

I was a child of Obsidian and before that I had been a child of a Revolutionary soldier. Could I turn my back on this?

"Kadee?" Vance asked, concerned. He was waiting for an answer.

My thoughts were chasing each other in circles. "We should stay," I said.

I was scared, and I wanted to run, but running would make us helpless. If I woke up a few days from now and saw the forest burning, I would never forgive myself. If Midnight never fell, I would always wonder what might have happened if someone had been brave enough to help the one civilization with the nerve and power to stand up for themselves.

When Ashley pushed open one of the doors in the north wing, we stepped inside. Vance dismissed her as I looked around the room, which was as ostentatious as every other part of Midnight I had seen. The painting on the wall, which was titled *Naraka*, according to the plaque beneath it, depicted a hellish scene lorded over by a red-robed man with blazing eyes and skin the color of the sky before a storm.

I was horrified by the picture itself, but Vance's re-action was more personal. He knew the artist.

"I hate this place," I said, an understatement for which I had no better words, as Vance caressed the painting's slick wooden frame.

He jerked his hand back as if shocked by his own gesture, then matter-of-factly reached up, took the painting down from its hooks, and placed it on the floor facing the wall.

"Will we get in trouble for that?" I asked.

"Only if Lady Brina sees. We can put it back before we leave." He shrugged, too casually. "Did Ashley say anything interesting when you were alone with her?"

"She said we shouldn't trust Misha," I said. "She wouldn't tell me anything more, though."

"I don't trust her," Vance said immediately. "I trust you and Farrell, and I mostly trust Malachi, and . . . I more or less trust the others, but I'm reserving judgment even about them."

I felt as guilty as I did gratified to find myself on that list. He trusted me. More importantly, he felt the same way I did about Misha.

"There wasn't much else," I said. "She's obviously—" *Broken* was the word trainers used for a person who has been stripped of will, but I didn't want that word on my tongue. I wasn't even sure it was accurate. "Her mind isn't right. She says she knows we—I—the Obsidian guild put her here," I said, stammering as I tried not to include Vance in that crime, "but she acts like it is meaningless to her. I don't know how clearly she is able to think about anything."

"That might be all her warning means," Vance suggested. "She knows Misha was the reason for her own enslavement, so perhaps seeing her and then us triggered some garbled memory and a vague warning."

I nodded. Maybe that was all it had been: a traumatic memory rising to the surface of a damaged mind.

"Are you hungry?" Vance asked.

I nodded, grateful for the change of subject. Perhaps I should have been too horrified to even think of wanting food, but righteous indignation was a stupid reason for an empty belly.

"Is there any way to cook in here?" I asked, thinking about the supplies we had with us. There was no fire in this magically heated room. Making due with dry, uncooked trail rations wouldn't make me feel any better about facing the trainers again the next night.

Vance shook his head. "Guests aren't expected to cook," he said. "We can either order a meal to be prepared for us, or go to the kitchen on our own."

"Where's the kitchen?" I asked. I would willingly eat Midnight's food, which had practically been stolen from shapeshifters in the first place, but I didn't think I could stand to ask a slave to wait on me, which I assumed was what Vance meant when he said "order a meal."

"This way."

Vance led us confidently into the hall, then paused. I saw indecision cross his face, and I asked, "Do you *know* where the kitchen is?" It was probably an insulting question—even serpiente royals could locate the kitchen, though I was pretty sure none of them knew how to use it—but for all I knew, Vance hadn't been allowed to visit such a common place. The vampires hadn't wanted him to know too much, after all.

"It's in the south wing," he answered immediately, "so we have a choice. Would you rather go past the trainers' rooms or the slaves' cells?"

"This way," I said, turning away from the library and the areas we had seen earlier. I wanted to avoid the trainers for as long as I could.

I wasn't prepared.

We passed a guard as we entered the east wing, through a heavy door that was closed but unlocked, and then all hints of comfort disappeared. Plush woven carpets gave way to gray stone, worn smooth by centuries of hopeless feet. Where other halls had boasted artwork, wood paneling, and frescoes, here there was more stone, occasionally dotted with ominous iron brackets or bars. I did not want to consider their possible uses.

There were no doors to conceal the cells we passed.

Most cells had four beds, simple blankets, and occasionally a small table cluttered with some kind of project. One had a braided scraps rug, which was noteworthy enough that I couldn't help glancing inside. The two children within were at the age where they were probably just beginning to walk, which explained the rug. Jeshickah wouldn't want her possessions damaged by a fall on the stone floor.

There were no windows, and no artwork to make this cool, gray place less oppressive.

I would die in here, I thought as I caught sight of a young girl diligently working with needle and thread. Around her throat was a collar, as if she were little better than an animal. *I would simply fade and die. How do they survive?*

CHAPTER 18

WE TURNED A corner, and instead of a long expanse of cells, we were suddenly surrounded by the sounds and smells of work: the steady *whump-whump* of a loom from one room, the splash of steaming water being poured into a washtub, and the mouth-watering aroma of baking bread and what smelled like meat stew.

Probably not squirrel, I thought as I followed my nose. The only sound missing from this scene was that of chatty conversation. The voices I heard were soft, murmuring whispers, impossible to make out.

We had just reached the doorway of an immense kitchen when a cultured voice from farther down the hall said, "Excuse me?"

The man who had hailed us wasn't a vampire. *Serpiente?* I wondered. His fair skin, bright blue eyes, and dark hair would make sense for that breed, which meant he was probably one of the bloodtraitors who worked for Midnight.

"Could you help me with something?" he asked, when we both regarded him warily. Then he ducked back into the room he had come from.

I looked to Vance for guidance, but he had already stepped forward. "That's the infirmary," he explained.

Was the man a healer? If so, he was still a traitor, but at least he was using his skills to try to alleviate suffering.

Or prolong it, I thought darkly, *if you consider slaves better off dead.*

As I walked into that room, I was struck by the strangest sense of familiarity and nostalgia, though for a moment I didn't know why. A memory surfaced of my mother sitting next to me, singing and soothing my brow.

Vinegar, I thought, realizing the smells in the room had triggered the memory, *and hyssop.* My mother had been a nurse, and especially once I had become ill, our home had always smelled this way.

The pungent memory had distracted me from the man who had summoned us here, but a low whimper brought my attention back to him, and the child who lay on a cot in front of him. The young boy was unconscious, hunched into a ball, trembling. His eyes were swollen and his breath came in wheezes.

"What did they do to him?" I gasped, horrified. The boy

was about the age I had been when I was brought to Diente Julian Cobriana. How I had railed and whined, horrified by the palace, and all the strangers around me, with their bizarre looks and customs. What an ungrateful child I had been.

"What did who do?" the man asked. "No one did anything to him. He stuck his hand in a black widow's nest while getting preserves from the root cellar."

"He isn't collared," Vance observed. "Who is he?"

"His father is one of the guards here, but the boy doesn't seem to have inherited his father's shapeshifting abilities at all," the man answered. "That's why the spider bite is affecting him like it would a human. It's also why I think you can help me," he said, looking up directly at me. "You're a serpent, aren't you?"

It was hard to resist just saying, "Yes, I'll help!" when the child moaned, but I didn't want to agree to anything until I knew what I was getting myself into. "Who are you?" I asked.

"My name is Stefan," the man answered. "I'm a witch, occasionally in Midnight's employ. Are you or aren't you? If you are, I can use you to trigger his shapeshifting reflex. It should purge the poison from his body, and save him a lot of trouble later."

"You can do that?" I asked. The Shantel had struggled for weeks when they tried to force me to shapeshift, and that was after my serpent form had tried to manifest on its own. Years later, I still found shapeshifting uncomfortable, and tried to do it as rarely as possible.

"If you're willing to help me."

"I'm only half serpent," I admitted. "Is that a problem?"

"What about his father?" Vance asked, his distrust clear in his voice. I was so concerned for the child, I had almost forgotten he was still there.

"So is he," the witch answered me, "it's fine." To Vance, he added, "His father is working in the market. The boy was brought in by one of the avian guards."

"What do you need me to do?" I didn't care that the child's father was a bloodtraitor, and quite possibly worse, since his human mother was probably a slave. A child wasn't responsible for the sins of his parents.

"I just need a little blood," Stefan said.

"Is this safe for Kadee?" Vance asked.

"Nothing I do will injure her," Stefan assured the quetzal. "I need far less than you gave to the vampires every time you let them feed."

He turned back to me too quickly to see the way Vance's gaze dropped at the reminder. I knew Vance's blood was what had infected the vampires, but I had never stopped to think *how*. They had fed on him. Stefan's words implied that Vance had been willing, but Vance's expression now spoke of shame.

Stefan was oblivious, too focused on the sick child and

the task at hand. He smoothed the child's flushed brow and said, "I understand your caution, but we are in a bit of a hurry. If you won't help, I should go find someone who will before it's too late. If it isn't already."

"Do what you need to do," I said. I held out my hand, and the witch drew a strange knife from a sheath at his waist. The handle looked like silver, but the blade was transparent, like glass, with a pink tint, as if it had already tasted blood.

The Shantel deathwitch who had nearly killed the trainers had also had a special knife, though his had been made of wood and inscribed with symbols. I was sure I wasn't the only one recalling that memory; I could almost feel Vance's tension vibrating in the air.

"What kind of witch are you?" I asked as the witch uncurled my palm and drew the blade across it. Either the blade was too sharp to hurt or the magic numbed the pain, because all I felt was a vague sense of warmth and tingling.

"Shhh," Stefan hushed me. He sheathed the knife, then turned my hand and let my blood drip into his curled palm, gathering it. His gaze went distant, the way Malachi's did when he was working magic or staring at visions, and I went silent.

The blood should have spilled through his fingers, but instead, it drew together in a sphere that he cradled in his hand like a bubble. The cut on my hand drew closed with a deep itching sensation as the witch reached his free hand out to the boy. Stefan gently touched the red, swollen fingers near the spider bite, and the inflamed flesh started to pale. He touched the child's temple, then his throat, and unbuttoned his shirt one-handed to place a palm over the boy's heart.

The boy gave a sharp, gasping breath, and I saw the witch's muscles tense as if he were *pushing* against the child's chest—but if he had actually applied that much force, the boy would have gone sailing off the other edge of the cot.

The child's skin writhed and rippled. I saw green-gray snakeskin appear and disappear in patches, like dappled sunlight coming through trees.

The boy's body started to shake, and I instinctively reached forward, catching the back of his head just in time to have my fingers slammed into the cot hard enough to bruise. Without needing to be told, Vance jumped forward to help hold the child's legs as his whole body began to seize.

This is what I looked like, I thought. The pain in one hand, the bone-deep itch in the other, the nostalgic smells of disinfectant and herbs, and the reality of watching this witch do for this child what no one had been able to do for me made my head spin.

The boy never stilled, but his body began to flow, shifting from a human child to a skinny green snake with white markings down its back. I pushed Vance away, unsure if this boy might be poisonous, but the snake just dropped its head and collapsed, tongue flickering slowly.

The witch let out a long, shaking breath, and wiped sweat from his brow. Then he reached forward, tapped the snake once on the head, and abruptly the boy returned. The swelling was gone, and the boy's skin had returned to a healthy color. He yawned widely and closed his eyes as the witch whispered, "Sleep, boy. You need rest."

"The Shantel weren't able to do that," I whispered, amazed.

Stefan raised a brow, almost appearing offended. "I've been studying my craft a good deal longer than any Shantel. I should hope I can do things they can't." He stood and stretched. "I don't suppose you would allow me to purchase some of your blood for future work?" he asked. "I could do a lot of good with it."

"There are other serpents here I'm sure you could deal with," I said, wary. We had healed the child, but I didn't want to fool myself into thinking this man was only a healer.

"Your half-human heritage is less common," Stefan explained. "Well, there's the boy, but I don't approve of bleeding small children, even if it *is* perfectly safe. And of course, *your* blood could be even more valuable," he added, looking back at Vance. "As you might imagine, the Azteka usually won't sell."

"They consider blood sacred," Vance said.

"But you and I know it's simply another commodity," Stefan replied. "I could compensate you in coin or craft. I'm aware that the Obsidian guild has their own witch, but I'm sure there are useful charms I could provide."

"What kind of work do you do?" I asked. He might be able to provide us with a valuable trade, but how dangerous could Vance's blood be in this man's hands?

"Hmm, what might appeal to a child of Obsidian?" he pondered aloud. "Perhaps a charm for warmth. I usually work them into doorways or thresholds, but I could etch one into a talisman you could carry with you, which would warm an area even if you could not light a fire. I could charm your bow to make sure your arrows fly true even in the wind. Or, if you're wary of magic, I have other resources. I am allowed a certain number of deer from Midnight's land, for example, and would be willing to trade some of that allowance."

All of that sounded good, but hadn't answered the question I tried to ask: *What will you do with Vance's blood?* His boast about the Shantel made me want to know one thing in particular.

"Serpents *like* fire," I said, trying to show the same reserve I would in the marketplace while trying to bargain for a better price. "I'm not sure they would bother with a charm that made warmth without flame. Now, if you could make a fire that would burn in the rain, on wet wood, *that* might be valuable."

"Making wood burn, even in the rain, is easy. Let me use *Vance's* blood," Stefan replied, "and I can make you a spark that will burn stone."

That's what I was afraid of, I thought. Even without Vance's blood, I believed this man posed a threat to the Shantel woods. At the moment he was dealing with us, and earlier he had been working to save a child, but the fact that he was here meant he worked for Midnight. *At least we have a real threat to report to the sakkri, in case she still doesn't believe they are in danger.*

"It's a tempting offer, but I don't sell my blood," Vance said. "I learned the hard way that it can have . . . unforeseen consequences."

"I heard you nearly killed all the trainers," Stefan answered, his voice almost jovial. "I would have paid a dear price to see that."

I didn't trust him enough to reply in any way. "I'm glad the boy is doing better," I said. "We'll be on our way now."

"Look me up if you change your mind, either of you," he said. He picked the boy up, cradling him in strong arms, and preceded us out of the room. Vance and I gave him a few minutes to get ahead of us before we left.

We picked up food at the kitchen as hastily as we could, then retreated to our room. I forced myself to eat, even though I had never felt less interested in food in my life. I wanted to curl up under open stars and free skies. These stone walls reminded me of the serpiente palace, without the comforting nooks and crevices where one could find peace.

When it came time to sleep, I feared I would have nightmares about children raised in cold gray cells.

And Shane will be there to play music for them, I thought darkly, and then shuddered.

"Are you all right?" Vance asked.

"Just tired."

"Where do you want to sleep?"

The choices were a giant, four-poster bed piled high with soft sheets and down blankets and pillows, a velvet upholstered couch, or, of course, the rug, which was so thick and plush it sank under my feet. There were other options—the claw-foot bathtub in the separate washroom was probably also large enough to sleep in—but even though I was used to the ground, I drew the line at cast iron for a bed.

"If—" I drew a deep breath to gather the nerve to ask Vance a question that would have been perfectly ordinary and acceptable for any normal serpiente but was more complicated between us. I didn't want Vance to get the wrong impression now in either direction: that I wanted more than his friendship tonight, or that I didn't trust the strength of that friendship. "If I say that I would really like you to hold me so I don't need to sleep alone, and that's *all* I want, is that all right?"

Most serpiente men had a little trouble with that line.

They might say yes, but twenty minutes later they would ask for more. I'd lost friends when I was younger who walked away from me, hurt and angry, when I drew a line between *friends* and *lovers*. Vance, on the other hand, had always been a gentleman. We had snuggled together under the trees plenty of times, and drifted off to sleep in each other's arms, but that hadn't involved a *bed*. Beds changed things.

Vance let his breath out in a rush, and he said, "As long as you hold me, too."

I hadn't slept in a real bed since I had fled the palace, but Vance's arms comforted me enough that I could begin to relax despite the weight of the day's events and the expectations of tomorrow. "I do miss beds," I admitted as we curled up together on the soft mattress.

"I miss pillows," Vance answered, snagging one to tuck beneath his head. "Soft, down pillows, instead of a rolled-up sack of supplies."

"Down?" I teased. "You're a *bird*."

"I'm not a goose," Vance replied magnanimously.

I rested my head on his shoulder, so the sound of his breathing and his heart filled the silence that otherwise ruled this stone place.

Somehow, I managed to slide into sleep.

I was hiding in one of the secret rooms that only I used to know. In real life, no one had ever found me there, but in the dream, guards dragged me out. They threw me to the floor in the royal receiving room, and told me to kneel to the Naga and Diente.

"A child of Obsidian kneels to no one," I said, defiantly coming to my feet.

In front of me stood Misha. She was wrapped in silver, gold, and jewels.

I heard Malachi's prophecy: "When you and your king rule, you will bow to no one. And this place, this Midnight, will burn to ash." The words rose up from the ground like an accusation.

Misha turned and took her mate's arm. Gabriel Donovan looked down at me with Cobriana-scarlet eyes. Misha's outfit of precious metals, I suddenly realized, wasn't a gown, but rather an endless series of chains. Gabriel held the end of her leash in his hand.

Around me, the firestorm began.

CHAPTER 19

IT WAS A LONG DAY.

Vance and I snacked on the supplies we had when we got hungry, but chose not to leave our room again until it was time to meet the vampires. We agreed that we would leave Midnight immediately after the meeting, regardless of the outcome, even if that meant traveling in the dark in order to find a suitable campsite. We would do what we could do for the Shantel, then put our backs to this place.

Lost in my musings, I nearly leapt out of my skin when the knock came at the door. When I answered, the same collared young man who had served tea the evening before informed us that Mistress Jeshickah would see us now.

"Thank y—"

I didn't get through my polite reply before Vance

grabbed my shoulder and hauled me back. "Kadee, *look* at him."

His posture was hunched and his gaze had been down until that moment, when he looked at Vance with confusion. His irises were perfectly jet-black. I stepped closer, horrified by what I already guessed to be true. He wasn't breathing. His face was utterly without expression, but his skin was chalky. There was no color in his dead cheeks.

"He's—" My voice choked off as I imagined an eternity as a mindless slave. "How . . ."

"Is this why they made us wait a day?" Vance choked out.

The slave—the *vampire* who had been a slave just the day before and was still wearing a slave's uniform and collar— answered obligingly, "Perhaps, sir. Mistress Jeshickah did say something to that effect."

I swallowed tightly. *"Why?"* I asked.

The slave's gaze dropped again. "I'm sorry, my lady, I do not know that."

If he was a vampire, could he still even be a slave? Obviously *he* thought so. Everyone said a broken slave could never be fixed. What was his purpose?

"I'm sorry to rush you," the slave added as I stared at him, "but my mistress is waiting."

I nodded. "Let's go," I said to Vance. "If he's a threat, I'm sure they will explain it to us."

Jeshickah was already seated at the head of the table

when we entered. She looked pale and drawn, but wore a satisfied smile.

Her entourage was significantly smaller than last night. The vampire-slave who had led us here crossed the room and knelt beside his mistress's chair, next to a young woman who had already assumed the same posture. I couldn't see her eyes, but I was almost certain that she was a vampire as well. The trainers were absent, but had been replaced by another man I recognized.

"Good evening Kadee, Vance," Stefan greeted us.

"Evening, Stefan," Vance replied. "May I say it is *not* a surprise to see you here?"

The witch chuckled, and then tossed a small bag toward us. I caught it reflexively before it would have hit my face. "For your assistance last night," he said. "A few coins from the shapeshifter whose son you helped save, and a very special piece of flint from me. It won't work long—two or three times, depending on what you are trying to burn—but I assure you it should light your campfire regardless of the wood's condition."

"Be sure to test it when you take our deal back to the Shantel," Jeshickah purred, the smile on her face cold enough to make me shiver.

My hand clenched the small bag, which was not really a payment. It was a warning. They wanted to prove they had the power to follow through on their threat if the Shantel continued to defy them.

"You should also tell them about Isaac and Ariadne here," she said, gesturing to the two vampires kneeling beside her. "Changing them both took quite a bit out of me," Jeshickah said as I continued to stare in horror at the collared vampire, "but he and Ariadne will be useful when we receive payment from the Shantel. Do you like their names?"

What kind of absurd question was *that*?

Vance cleared his throat, and said, "Ariadne . . . King Minos's daughter. She supervised the labyrinth where sacrifices were brought to the Minotaur, until she helped Theseus defeat it."

I didn't know that tale, but the word *sacrifices* had triggered another old memory. "Isaac was . . ." The memory was so faint. I knew there was more to the biblical story, but all I could recall was, "bound by his father, to be sacrificed."

"Given the events that led us here, I thought it wise to take some precautions. *My* Isaac and Ariadne will be sacrificed, too, if necessary. They're . . . food tasters, so to speak, and if one of them so much as *sneezes* after spending some time with my new Shantel acquisitions, I will consider any deal we make invalid, and proceed with my original plan. Is that clear?"

I nodded. Shantel magic had made Vance's blood poisonous, and nearly killed four of Jeshickah's elite, chosen trainers. Isaac and Ariadne were protection against a double cross using a similar method. Suddenly I very much hoped the Shantel had been honest. I doubted these were the only precautions Midnight had taken.

"Shall we get down to business?" Jeshickah asked. "Please, take a seat. Isaac, scribe the meeting for us," she ordered, causing the slave to bounce to his feet and sit at a nearby desk. "Since you are negotiating for an absent party, it is polite to put any terms we agree to on paper. You will of course have a chance to review the document before giving it to the Shantel, to ensure everything is in order."

She knows we can't read, I thought as I watched Isaac prepare paper, pen, and ink.

I felt like we had already lost a fight, and we hadn't even reached our chairs yet.

Vance and I both sat. I had a feeling that any "negotiation" we had intended was already essentially over. How could the two of us have thought we could make any headway against this group of immortals?

Jeshickah laced her fingers together on the table, and then summarized our offer.

"It is my understanding that the Shantel have offered their prince Shane as full payment for their debt. This *might* have been considered sufficient if we had heard from them more promptly and apologetically, but considering the time that has passed, the disruption to market trade during these last months, and the cost we've incurred just to ensure that *any* payment be made, the Shantel can hardly expect us to accept one young man as adequate compensation.

Given your persuasive arguments last night, however, I am willing to accept the young prince as partial payment, and discuss how else to satisfy the debt."

I gritted my teeth. We had expected this, but I didn't know how to proceed. I hoped Vance was feeling a little more confident. He said, "Tell us what you're asking."

"I had initially asked for two trained witches to cover the human property lost in the plague. I am willing to accept that Shane has magical training, but I still want a fully trained witch. I don't care which sex as long as he or she is young—less than twenty-five years. *Additionally,* the Shantel lose all the extra privileges I have allowed them in the past. When it comes time to balance their accounts, their prince or king will come to us just as the serpiente and avians always have. We are done begging to enter their forest when we must conduct business. If they are *ever* late when accounts are due, and we must go to them, we will demand flesh in payment. Finally, they must stop barring our people from their land, and their merchants must return to the marketplace, with an increased tax on goods sold there until such time as they have repaid the cost of cleaning their space in the market, and the lost profits from the past four months."

"You mean, until *you* decide," I said, imagining Midnight holding this deal over the Shantel for generations.

"We can provide an itemized account so the payments can be clearly tracked," Jeshickah replied immediately.

The response took me aback. I had expected her to challenge me, just to be cruel or petty. People said that Midnight was a business and Jeshickah prioritized trade as much as she expected everyone else to, but I hadn't really believed it.

I bit my lip, made myself stop as soon as I noticed, and decided, *Fine. She responded to that challenge as if I were intending to bargain. She didn't even seem angry that I had spoken up. If this is a negotiation . . . what can I get?*

"You say you have lost profits, but the Shantel haven't benefited from Midnight these past four months either," I pointed out. "They haven't used your markets, your messengers, or even your roads. They haven't purchased any of your goods. What profits do they owe you on goods and services they haven't used?"

The Obsidian guild didn't pay taxes because we didn't use most of Midnight's services: we did not buy their food, have dedicated space in their markets, or use their roads to transport heavy carts full of trade goods through the forest. We were even careful not to spend more time on their land than we needed to in order to trade. The way the laws were written, if a shapeshifter nation was willing to forego everything Midnight offered—including an alternative to starving to death, for most of them—they didn't technically *owe* the vampires anything.

Jeshickah paused, considering the point. "That argument has been made before," she said. A smile touched her lips, as if she knew something I did not know—one thing on a long list, I was sure—and then she nodded. "I will concede that they do not owe *additional* taxes on the four months they have been absent, but they do still owe interest on late payments from previous fees, as well as the fee for cleaning their area of the market, and the location of the meeting where such payments are made—on *my* land, not theirs—is not negotiable."

I had accomplished something, I supposed, by cutting out a bit of the money the Shantel owed. I honestly didn't care if the Shantel paid their taxes in their woods or Midnight's market, so I had no interest in arguing that point. That left the vilest part of this arrangement still untouched. I didn't have the language to argue the cost of a soul the same way I had assessed the value of coins.

I looked to Vance. Among the Shantel, he had demonstrated his ability to engage in this discussion. Either he took my glance as a cue, or my speaking up had emboldened him, because he drew a deep breath and said, "That means the flesh you're asking for is entirely meant to pay for the original attack. You were willing to accept two blood-witches from the Azteka, correct?"

"One shapeshifter for each human death, or one trained, adult witch for every ten."

"How can you justify asking for a shapeshifter to pay for a human?"

My stomach twisted. I wanted to protest that a human

was no less valuable than a shapeshifter. My mother, my father—they weren't less precious than a serpent or avian. I bit my lip only because I knew Vance was arguing for us, and had to use language Jeshickah understood.

"The humans we lost were either broken slaves or second-generation slaves bred in Midnight," Jeshickah replied. "Time and resources went into their creation." Offhand, she added, "If you had access to any, I suppose I would accept humans for half the payment, or even a single shapeshifter of any age or magical aptitude, if you were willing to work to make up the difference."

Vance recoiled, falling back in his seat.

"No?" Jeshickah asked. "Well, I'll be sure to include the offer when I write our agreement out for the Shantel. Otherwise, we're back to a son of the royal house, plus a trained, healthy witch of childbearing age ... or I suppose Shane, plus any ten nonmagical Shantel they choose to send."

Vance had gone pale, and instead of responding, he swallowed tightly. Jeshickah had just given the Shantel permission to sell *him* as the second part of the payment, and made it clear that she would put the offer in writing, where we wouldn't be able to conceal it.

"You should know," I said, "that part of our arrangement with the Shantel was that, if we agreed to negotiate this deal, they would grant our guild the same privileges and protections as your mercenaries."

I would have liked to think the Shantel *wouldn't* sell Vance, even to protect their own people, as long as he dealt fairly with them. It was even better to know they *couldn't* sell him, according to Midnight's own laws.

"What a pity," Jeshickah replied, though she didn't sound particularly disappointed. I hoped that meant her words had been a gambit to unsettle Vance, instead of a serious desire.

She wouldn't have offered unless she was serious, I thought. *If the Shantel had taken her up on it, she would have been obliged to accept a deal she had proposed.*

"I will see that my men are informed, and keep it in mind for future negotiations," Jeshickah said, again with a hint of a smile. "I will consider that deal binding from the moment we conclude our discussion here, and you agree to carry my offer back to the Shantel. That should protect your Vance in the way you wish without complicating any other business. Is that acceptable?"

I looked to Vance nervously, sure there was some meaning in those words that I didn't understand. Vance asked, "Am I correct that this would make the Obsidian guild unable to sell any freeblood shapeshifter, and unable to be sold by any nation?"

"No nation may sell one of our employees for profit," Jeshickah corrected, "but if you are foolish enough to be arrested in their land—say by the serpiente, for crimes against their throne—they are still within their rights to decide your fate. Otherwise, you are correct."

No wonder Vance had been willing to risk so much. He had understood the implications of this deal even better than I did. Not only did it make it impossible for us to trade in innocent flesh ever again, as we had when we sold Alasdair, but it also made it more difficult for Midnight to acquire us.

"Can we get back to business?" Jeshickah suggested.

My spirit was buoyed slightly by what I saw as a success: Vance, at least, was safe. In fact, all of our guild was suddenly safer—at least in Midnight's land—than we ever had been before.

Using my renewed confidence, I said, "The Shantel say you already took one of them, a merchant named Amber, when she came here to negotiate. Doesn't she count as—as partial payment?"

"Amber did not come here to *negotiate*," Jeshickah replied dismissively. "She came here to repeat the insulting offer the Shantel had been trying to make for months. When she heard our counteroffer, she became violent, and in doing so relinquished her freeblood status. I am willing to consider her actions the ill-advised, impulsive protest of an individual, but if the Shantel want her to apply to their account, then they can claim culpability in that assault as well."

"No!" I gasped. We were trying to *help* the Shantel, not get them in even more trouble. "The Family just knew Amber had been taken, nothing else. They aren't responsible." *Though they might be proud,* I thought.

Jeshickah nodded. "Then we're agreed that her status has nothing to do with our current negotiations."

I looked at Vance again, searching for help, and instead found inspiration.

"How much did it cost for you to raise Vance here so his quetzal blood wouldn't kill him?" I asked. Vance hadn't been raised in the stone cells I had seen because a quetzal couldn't survive in a cage.

"Is that relevant right now?" Jeshickah asked.

"When you asked for two bloodwitches, you knew that any Azteka sold to you, or born here, is as likely to be a quetzal as a jaguar. A Shantel child *will* have magic, regardless of his parents' training or lack, but will not cost you as much to raise as an Azteka could." Dear God, was I really talking about raising an infant in this terrible place? The only way I could even keep speaking was by picturing the trainers the way they had looked when the deathwitch's spell had been on them. We had nearly killed them all once. We could do it again. "Did you factor those future savings into the price you are asking?"

"It's a pity you're so squeamish," Jeshickah remarked. "You have a head for economics. Fine, I will adjust the requirements for the second half of the payment. As long as the individual I receive is healthy and relatively young, that will be sufficient to cover the loss of property, but if they send me a witch, I will consider that sufficient to cover the owed fees as well." I drew breath to reply, and she said, "That is my final offer. Take it to the Shantel. My mercenaries inform me that, with Shantel consent, it should take no more than two days to reach the Family Courtyard from the edge of their land. Therefore, I will give the Shantel one week from today to deliver payment.

"If they do not agree to these terms, they may buy themselves time by delivering Shane along with their counteroffer. If I hear nothing, or they waste my time with more foolish delays, I will be forced to take stronger measures. If it looks like the Shantel intend to dally and bicker, I recommend you two exit the forest immediately, because I cannot guarantee your safety should you stay."

She pushed herself to her feet, prompting Isaac and Ariadne to stand with her, and snapped, "Dismissed now, all of you. I have work to do."

She swept out of the library before Vance and I had found our feet. Ariadne trailed after her, but Isaac took a few more moments to sand and seal the notes he had taken, and give them to us before he followed the others out.

My legs felt like they had turned to water. I let out a slow breath, and jumped as Stefan spoke up, saying, "Farrell and Malachi Obsidian can be fickle masters, but they have obviously taught you some valuable skills. If you ever tire of them, you should come here. You could do well."

At that, he, too, left us, so Vance and I were alone with our pounding hearts and perspiration.

"That went . . ." I trailed off.

"Better than it had a right to," Vance said. "Do you think she's always that reasonable, or did she let us win because she wants to encourage us to come back?"

"I wouldn't call that *winning*," I replied. The concessions we had earned felt like things we hadn't even realized were being demanded. I hadn't really believed we could protect Shane, but I had hoped they were right that we could protect *someone*. Now we were still left going back to the Shantel and telling them that not only did they need to send Shane, they also needed to choose another victim to send into the spider's nest.

Would they agree? More importantly, would the sakkri agree? If she didn't, how much would Vance and I be risking by going back into the Shantel woods? The deadline Jeshickah had given didn't leave any room for hesitation.

CHAPTER 20

WE HAD BARELY passed outside Midnight's black gates before I saw a flash of white wings. Malachi looked relieved as he appeared in front of us and said, "We're camped less than an hour from here. This way."

My first thought upon seeing Malachi wasn't the joy of reunion, but the memory of the cells we had seen in the east wing. A dozen half-formed thoughts bubbled to the surface of my mind, but none of them seemed appropriate to ask.

How did you survive?

Vance's thoughts had traveled further. "We saw Misha last night. What—" Vance broke off, as if worried about sounding too suspicious of Malachi's sister. "Is she all right?"

Malachi nodded with a grin that didn't seem to match Misha's condition when last I'd seen her.

"We were all worried about you two alone in Shantel land. Misha went to Midnight to try to get an official word on what was going on with the Shantel. I was glad when she said she saw you and you were safe, but then you never came back out. I've been circling this area ever since."

Was that how Misha told the story?

Was that the "favor" she had asked—nothing more than news about us?

It could be. Misha had probably made the offer in her ongoing, desperate quest to conquer her fears, just as she had when she decided to go to the market. Unfortunately, it was not hard to imagine that she had returned to the vampires to ask a question, and had ended up manipulated into much more by the man who had held and abused her for months. In that case it was also easy to imagine why she had been so angry to see us. She had probably blamed us for putting her in that situation.

"Are you two all right?" Malachi asked as he started to lead the way through the woods.

"We are," I answered. "We need to get back to the Shantel soon, though."

"The camp isn't far from here," Malachi answered. "You'll make better time if you sleep tonight and move on in the daylight. And . . . well, there's something you should see." He shook his head, sending white hair rippling.

We entered the camp to find a roaring fire in the center, and all of our kin surrounding it . . . along with two serpiente royal guards, one of whom had recently had a bow pointed at me. The man, Liam, was the one the commander had told to get "his" Arami. They were both sitting somewhat stiffly, unarmed, across the fire from their prince.

Aaron was seated at Farrell's left with Misha half beside him, and half in his lap. And she was *laughing*, her eyes bright and her voice cheerful for the first time since we had brought her back to us. No wonder Malachi had grinned when we asked how she was.

Vance and I exchanged a glance as Malachi went to Farrell's side. The three rose to greet us. Misha wrapped me in a warm hug that made me tense with confusion.

"Kadee, I'm so glad you're all right," she said. "I'm sorry I was sharp with you when I saw you last. I was"—the open, welcoming smile flickered briefly, but I couldn't make out the expression that tried to emerge before it was hidden again—"not myself. That place . . ."

Around us, the others nodded sympathetically. Aaron stepped forward and wrapped a comforting arm around Misha's waist. Was it my imagination, or did she flinch first before leaning against him? Shapeshifters healed fast, but I wondered if she still wore bruises under her clothes.

"What did Midnight say about the Shantel situation?" Aaron asked us.

"Aaron," I said, my eyes going from Farrell Obsidian—one of the most wanted outlaws in serpiente history—to the royal guards Aaron had brought with him. "What . . ."

I could not even form the question, but Aaron guessed it.

"Naomi and Liam are personal friends of mine," he told me. "They are here not as my guards, but as individuals who support me, and so will support you. Malachi assures me he would never have let them cross into this camp if he had not been able to guarantee their loyalty."

Farrell spoke up. "I can understand why you are nervous, Kadee," he said. "I was concerned myself at first. They have both willingly relinquished their weapons."

I nodded, though I wasn't entirely convinced. Aaron had tried to be kind to me in the palace, and I appreciated that, but I couldn't help remembering how naive he had been about what life was like for a half-human girl among the serpiente. He had never really understood why I cried when a male friend suddenly decided he wasn't satisfied being *friends*, or when one of the royal guards decided I was the source of all his problems. Aaron didn't know what it meant to be lonely or afraid.

Or hunted.

"Your being here is not going to improve your chances at the crown," I said. I could not find it in me to welcome Aaron, or to curse him. He might have saved my life earlier, but that didn't mean I had to trust him—especially when I didn't understand what was going on now.

Aaron just shook his head and glanced at Misha before he said, "It doesn't matter."

"It doesn't *matter*?" Vance echoed.

"Julian has decided," Aaron said. "He is going to announce his heir at the Brysh-diem, in one month, and I have reason to believe I am his choice."

"*You?*" I asked. "You're the younger child, and you're not even *his*."

"Hara is hotheaded and self-centered."

"That describes most serpents," Vance replied drily.

Aaron nodded with a half smile, acknowledging the point. Quick-sparking tempers were nothing unusual among the serpiente. It certainly would not be enough to convince a father to deny his only daughter her rightful place on the throne.

"Just . . . trust me," Aaron said. "I can't go into all the details, but Hara is not in good graces with her father right now."

"You didn't tell us any of this earlier," I said.

"We didn't have a chance for extended conversation," Aaron pointed out. "Let's just say that Midnight would love for Hara to take the throne. She follows her father's policy of playing nice and staying passive. I do not think they will be very happy after they hear what Julian has to say."

I'm not ready for this, I thought.

What if Aaron *did* become king? The way Misha was hanging on him made it clear that she would make her way to the throne beside him, bringing that part of Malachi's prophecy to fruition. Then Aaron would take the throne, and ... and *what?* What would happen to the Obsidian guild, if Farrell Obsidian's son ruled?

We had worked for this, sacrificed for it, but I realized in that moment that I had never really believed it would happen. A white viper on the serpiente throne—impossible!

My head was tied up in knots. Vance stayed by the fire, and I heard Malachi asking him what had happened with the Shantel. I made an excuse to get away from Aaron, who went back to snuggling with Misha.

Farrell sought me out in my solitude.

"I imagine this is a shock for you."

Cliché and understatement.

"It was a shock for me as well," Farrell said. "I knew Aaron was my son, but a long time ago I accepted that he would always call Julian Cobriana his father. I considered speaking to him a thousand times, but always came to the conclusion that even if I could reach him without the guards capturing me, his adoptive father had doubtless poisoned his opinion of me."

"How did Misha manage to speak to him?" I asked. I didn't doubt that she could sneak into the palace if she wanted to, but surely Aaron would have summoned guards the moment he saw a white viper.

"I don't really know," Farrell answered. "At great risk, I'm sure, but after what she has been through, I do not think she is able to fear anything anymore. She knew what a reunion with Aaron would mean to me." He paused, and added significantly, "And I know what the serpiente royal house means to you. Please, Kadee, try to keep an open mind. Aaron is my son, and Misha has spent the last weeks teaching him our ways. He considers you a sister, not a subject. I hope you will be able to see him as a brother, not a king you must fight."

"How can one of us be a king?" I demanded. It was one thing to talk about Midnight burning, or even about Misha becoming queen. That was prophecy; it was abstract and far away, talk of "someday" and "imagine when." This was sudden, immediate, and came with *royal guards* sitting in our camp. "How can he be one of us and be on the throne? Isn't it everything we stand against?"

Farrell smiled sadly. "In that way, he is Julian's son. When he appeared in our camp, I will admit I had a brief fantasy that he had decided to join us completely, but he has never spoken a word that indicates he has even considered anything other than taking the throne."

"What will you do?" I asked. "Will you call him king?"

I didn't just ape Obsidian ideals because I had nowhere else to go. I truly believed in them, and they said that it was our responsibility not to rule and not to let ourselves be ruled. I held no hatred for Aaron, but the idea of Farrell bowing before him disgusted me.

"I will call him son," Farrell answered. "And you will call him brother, and unless I am mistaken, Misha will call him husband. And if he really does speak up against

Midnight, as he intends, I will call him brave, and a hero, and I will pray that they allow him to live."

"Do you really think it can happen?" I asked, my voice shaking a little. What I had seen inside Midnight proper flashed before my eyes. Children living in cells. Collars around throats too pale to have ever seen the sun. Jeshickah's face as she calmly bartered with us. Misha's injuries as she snarled at the trainer. Alasdair, now stripped of even her name, as docile as a doll as she obeyed her master's commands. "Can Misha destroy Midnight?"

"I have staked the last two decades of my life on that belief," Farrell answered. "I lost Aaron's mother over it. I accepted every vile thing the Cobriana said about me, and let them tarnish my name, because I believed Malachi when he told me his mother was with child, and that child would grow up to change this world."

"The Shantel seem to know something about the prophecy," I said. I was still confused and overwhelmed by what I had seen tonight—it seemed so sudden and inexplicable— but I would not hide information from Farrell. He had given more than any of us to our cause. I told him the gist of what had happened in Shantel land, including the brief conversation I had overheard between Shane and the sakkri about how the "white queen" would not rise in time to save him if he went to Midnight.

Farrell's eyes widened, and the expression I saw on his face was joyous. "A falcon prophecy shows what *could* be, not what must be, but they say that a Shantel prophecy is always true. Are you and Vance going back?"

"Do you think we should?" I asked. Vance and I had already decided to go, but I still wanted to hear Farrell's opinion.

I expected him to say, *It's up to you,* but instead, he spoke with a fanatic's voice. "If you do, you might be able to press them for more details of their prophecy about the white queen."

"Maybe," I said. I didn't want to know more about the prophecy. If the Shantel said Misha would take the throne, then she would, right? There was nothing we could do to ensure or endanger that future.

That was a relief, because I had already done more than I could stand. I wanted out of this juggernaut before we were asked to sacrifice another Alasdair, another Shane.

When the others began to dance to the accompaniment of a flute played by Aaron's guard Liam, Farrell returned to the group. My kin knew me well enough that they did not question my decision not to join them . . . except for Vance, who came to sit beside me, and said, "Your face is hard to read when you want it to be."

I shrugged.

"I can read you anyway," Vance added. "You would be comfortable if he were one of us, and called you a sister, or if he was king, and called you a villain. Can you accept a king who calls you a sister?"

I threw a halfhearted glare his way. "He is the closest thing to a brother I have ever had, but accepting him, and forgiving him . . . I want to, but I don't know if I can."

"What do you need to forgive him for?"

"Nothing," I answered.

"You're the one who used the word," Vance pointed out.

"I'm not saying 'nothing' because I just don't want to talk," I snapped. "I mean, he didn't actually *do* anything that anyone wouldn't have done. He didn't protect me when I was a child because he was still practically a child himself. He didn't understand what my life was like. But that sums it up, doesn't it? *He doesn't understand.* He is Farrell's son, but he will never understand what it means to *not* be a prince, a king. Do we expect that to change when he takes the throne?"

"He speaks of you as a sister," Vance said.

Was I being reasonable, or just being a faithless coward?

I bit my lip and admitted, "I do not want to think of him as a brother. Not when I know what Midnight might do to him."

Malachi said that Misha would become queen. Here she was, nice and friendly with the prince who said he was in line to become king. Shouldn't I take that, as impossible as it had once seemed, as a sign? Yet, when I imagined Aaron and Misha taking the throne, all I could see was the look on Shane's face when he said, *"I'm what we're offering."*

Midnight would make an example of the Shantel despite all their power. The serpiente had no magic forest to protect them.

As if summoned by my thought of him, Malachi joined us. His earlier smile had faded, and now he looked tired. "Are you two going to stay the night?" he asked.

I was grateful beyond words when Vance said, "I'm a little nervous about sleeping an arm's length away from palace guards."

"I'm surprised no one else is," I said, thinking about the others who had come north with Malachi and now seemed unusually content to camp on Midnight's land and break bread with serpiente guards.

"Legally, they cannot assault us here," Malachi said, though even he sounded unconvinced. He shook his head. "You two should go. I know I said you should come here, but perhaps you're right. You have other things to do, and distance from Misha would be good."

"From *Misha*?" I asked. The concerns we had expressed had been about the guards.

Malachi didn't clarify. Instead, he turned his back on us to return to the others.

Vance sighed. "If we're going to leave, we should get going," he said. "We still need some sleep before we tackle the Shantel forest."

I nodded, though my thoughts were less on the Shantel and more on Malachi's words. *Distance from Misha would be good.* What was he worried about?

CHAPTER 21

MY DREAMS THAT night were surreal.

I was on a bridge, looking at the rushing river running underneath. Water and foam sprayed into the air whenever the river struck one of the pillars holding up the bridge.

Where was I?

I looked to my left, and it seemed to be nighttime. On that side of the bridge stood Malachi, Vance . . . and Midnight's trainers. To my right were Misha and Aaron, almost wrapped around each other, kissing under a dawn that had streaked the sky red.

Not dawn, I realized. Fire. The fire started rushing toward the bridge. It engulfed Misha and Aaron, and then started to lick the wooden pilings of my bridge. Smoke filled my lungs, making me cough as I backed slowly across the bridge until I realized my only choices were to walk into that darkness—or dive into the water.

I put my hands on the rough wooden planks of the bridge, and was climbing onto the railing when arms wrapped around me, and Vance said, "It's okay, Kadee. It's—"

"It's okay." I opened my eyes, waking to the sound of Vance's voice. "You were having a nightmare. You're okay now."

Too many nightmares, I thought, trying to recall how many times lately I had woken to similar words, trying to scramble from nighttime horrors into a world that sometimes didn't seem much better.

Like in my dream, the sky above us was streaked violet and mauve. These clouds however were painted by the rising sun, not fire and smoke.

Vance yawned widely, which wasn't surprising. After saying goodbye to the others, we had traveled as far as we could stand before we set up our own camp and managed to get at most two or three hours of sleep.

"I have our bags packed already, except for your bedding," Vance said. He had apparently slept even worse than I had.

Packing took only a few moments, and then we were on our way toward Shantel land once again.

"What was the nightmare?" Vance asked.

I shook my head. The images were already fading, and it did not take a genius to understand where they had come from. I was worried about Aaron and Misha, and I was worried about what Midnight would do to us all. I did not want to face either fear, so in the dream I had decided to jump.

In real life, I didn't have that luxury. I wasn't the kind of person who could just run away from my problems, even if at the moment they seemed terrifying and insurmountable.

Some time away from the others might be good, I thought. If Misha and Aaron really did take the throne, I could be happy for them at a distance. Aaron had expressed an intention to ally with the Shantel to fight Midnight. If that happened, I would hear about it and could still be involved. And if Midnight crushed Aaron and Misha and all our hopes, I wouldn't be there to see it.

Maybe that was what Malachi meant. I needed distance from Misha and Aaron in order to wrap my mind around all the possibilities their relationship created.

Vance and I moved closer as we approached the edge of Shantel land. The air suddenly seemed colder, and thicker. Before when I had crossed into Shantel territory, I had a sense of welcome, as if no matter how I felt about it, the land still thought of me as a friend.

Not anymore.

"At least it probably won't try to keep us," Vance said under his breath. Gooseflesh was visible on his arms, and I could see the feathers at the back of his neck had lifted.

We pushed on. The forest had accepted our presence here, albeit grudgingly. Hopefully that meant it understood our purpose and was willing to let us accomplish it, not that it was going to drop us into a swamp or over a cliff.

"When this is over," Vance said hesitantly as we moved through the trees, "and we have done what we need to do for the Shantel . . . can we disappear for a little while?"

"Disappear to where?" I asked.

"Anywhere," Vance answered. "Whatever Aaron may be to you, he is nothing but a *prince* to me. He called them friends, but the people he brought with him to our camp were soldiers. I joined the Obsidian guild because I never wanted to be part of that again, on either side. I don't want to be his subject, or his guard, or his companion or cohort."

"Would you be interested . . ." I trailed off because the idea seemed stupid, but the curiosity in Vance's eyes made me continue. "Marcel said, if I wanted, she would take me to find my parents. I wouldn't stay there forever." Marcel was probably right that life as a human would be stifling after the relative freedom of a child of Obsidian. "But it would be nice to see where I came from one more time." I continued quickly, in case Vance had no interest at all in traveling with me to a human town, to meet humans who meant so much to me but nothing to him. "Regardless, I agree, I'm in no hurry to return to our would-be future queen."

The phrase slipped out, and then I bit my lip as I realized where I had heard it: Gabriel.

"I would be honored to meet your parents," Vance answered. In the reedy spring light filtering through the trees, his smile looked sad. "I wish I had someone like that, who I could look at and say 'That's where I came from. That's who made me who I am.'" Another pause, and in a dark attempt at humor, he added, "Someone who wasn't an evil, blood-drinking tyrant."

We kept moving, eating while we walked instead of stopping for lunch. Like Vance, I wanted to get this over with. If Marcel wouldn't take us to human lands, we would go somewhere else. We were the Obsidian guild's youngest members, but we weren't helpless. I couldn't tackle a bear like Aika could, or make a gourmet meal out of cornmeal and gathered roots like Torquil could, but Vance and I knew enough about hunting and gathering that we wouldn't starve.

You'll miss them, though.

Of course I would. I didn't intend to leave them forever—just long enough for fate to decide what to do about Aaron and Misha's bid for the throne, and for me to decide what I wanted to do about an Obsidian prince.

I kicked a pinecone in irritation. It flew up, startling Vance, and was caught by a Shantel guard.

"Finally," I whispered. They must have been shadowing us for hours, ever since we crossed into Shantel land. Now that they had shown themselves, we would probably make better time.

Their faces were grave, and they made no attempt to speak with us, only waved us ahead and then flanked us as we picked up the pace. They did not take our weapons away this time, which seemed like a good sign. We had threatened Shane in order to escape this forest, but surely it wouldn't have let us back in unless it knew we were here to try to help.

Not soon enough, we entered the Family home at suppertime. Prince Lucas looked up from a barely touched meal with resignation when we entered.

"My father is looking for Shane," he said. He added swiftly, "He isn't missing. He has taken to spending his evenings in the woods instead of his normal quarters, so it sometimes takes a little while to unearth him. I will admit, we did not think you would return. Did you make it to Midnight?"

"Barely," I answered, thinking of the way the forest had dumped us in the middle of serpiente royal guards. If that group had included Hara instead of Aaron, or if Aaron hadn't been quite as swayed by Misha's words about our guild, our story would have ended very differently.

"I'm sorry," Lucas answered. I suspected he knew exactly where we had ended up. "I am glad you are safe." The words were flawlessly polite, but his body vibrated with tension as he asked, "What did Midnight have to say?"

Vance handed him the sheath of papers from Jeshickah. "We convinced her to deal instead of just burning you out, but she didn't accept the deal you offered. This is her counteroffer. You have one week ... five days, now ... to send a reply."

Lucas skimmed the writing before him, eyes darting left and right as he tracked the letters that meant so little to me or Vance. As he read, Shane and their father entered the room. Shane's eyes were red as if from exhaustion. I doubted he had slept at all since we had last seen him, and though he shook my hand in greeting, he kept a wary distance from Vance.

Lucas's eyes narrowed. Had he come to the part about Jeshickah wanting a trained witch in addition to Shane?

"You must have expected something like this," Vance said.

"As a possibility, yes," Lucas answered, "but not a certainty." He gave the papers to his father, then reached out a hand to his brother's and squeezed it tightly.

Perhaps that was all the explanation Shane needed. He sat at the opposite end of the table without asking anything.

Lucas looked to his father as he said, "They aren't happy just pulling our family apart, or demanding that we sacrifice someone else. Half of this is dedicated to taxes and fees and trade requirements. Little humiliations, just in case forcing us to give them the flesh of our people isn't sufficient."

"*That* is what has you most upset?" I asked. I tried to remember the little details Jeshickah had mentioned. Something about coming to the market to balance accounts, instead of making the vampires come to them ... the little privileges that had kept the Shantel better off than the serpiente or avians. "You're preparing to send them your brother, but you're upset that they've insulted your pride?"

"You don't understand," Lucas said. "You've never needed to rule a people. What you call *pride* is the independence that gives us the power to protect those we serve."

There was no point in arguing. I wasn't one of his people, and I never would be.

"What kind of power does Midnight have on its side?" Lucas asked. "Can they do what they threaten?"

I pulled out the flint Stefan had given me and set it on the table. Just touching it made me feel grimy, and by the way the three Shantel men stared at it, I suspected whatever they felt was worse. Could they sense the magic in it?

"This was made by one of their witches. He claims it can burn just about anything. He encouraged us to have you test it."

None of them reached for the flint.

King Laurence swallowed audibly. "I will speak to the sakkri about choosing a second—"

"No!" both Shane and Vance insisted.

Laurence looked to Vance first, but spoke to his son. "How would you suggest we make this decision?"

"Ask for volunteers," Shane said. "Do not put this decision on the sakkri."

I suspected that Shane did not want them consulting with the sakkri for his own reasons, but I supported the notion. "If anyone goes to that place as a slave, it should be by their own decision, not at the will of their king or witch."

"Unless it was addressed in our absence," Vance added, "we still have a different problem. Kadee and I made it to Midnight, negotiated, and came to an agreement, but the deal is off if you cannot deliver on your side of the bargain."

"We have less than a week," Lucas informed Laurence and Shane, "to decide what we want to do, and send a reply—with payment—to Midnight."

"What I *want*," Laurence said, "is not to sacrifice *anyone*. I want to stand proudly, and tell Midnight that no, I will never give them one of my people. To tell them that we will not pay their taxes, or allow their mercenaries in our land. But the end result would be the slow death of all my people by starvation, or the kidnapping and enslavement of anyone Midnight can get its hands on . . . or the swift finality of fire."

His gaze fell to the flint in front of Lucas.

"So we compromise," Lucas said softly. "But I do not want the guards to feel obligated to volunteer themselves. They signed up to protect us, and to give their lives if the situation called for it, but none of them promised their souls."

"Agreed," Laurence said.

"You speak to the people and try to find a volunteer, then," Shane said. "I will tell the sakkri our decision, to make sure we can get out of this forest once an appropriate white lamb is found."

"Good idea," Laurence said. "I will speak to the head of the guard, and make it clear that I will not tolerate her pressuring any of her soldiers. We will all meet back here at dawn."

Are they all completely blind? I wondered, looking at Vance, who quirked a brow as if he knew exactly what was on my mind.

Shane knew why they couldn't get out of the forest. Were Laurence and Lucas still so utterly in the dark? How did they explain their inability to control their own forest—reluctance on the part of the royal family? If so, it was pure idealism that blinded them. They knew the rules about the sakkri that held her separated from them all and maintained her holiness. They obviously could not imagine that Shane could have committed such a powerful taboo.

After his brother and father left, Vance said to Shane, "I assume you have not told them about your affair with the sakkri."

"Let me speak to her alone," Shane pleaded. "I can make her understand what needs to be done. Please . . . you do not know what my family would say, if they knew I had—" He took a deep breath, and concluded simply. "I want them to remember me well. Please, leave me that."

"Convince the sakkri that Midnight is a threat. Show her this." I picked up the flint and pressed it into his hand. Shane tried to pull back, and I could see the hair on his arm raise as I closed his fingers around the flint. "I believe Midnight when they say they can burn your forest. You say you want your family to remember you well, but I am sure you do not want them all to die for you."

CHAPTER 22

AS EACH MEMBER of the royal family disappeared, Vance and I found ourselves strangely unchaperoned, an odd occurrence on Shantel land, and a somewhat disquieting one.

Leaving the Family home alone was perhaps unwise, but that only occurred to us after we had done so. Whereas the forest had seemed malevolent, the ground here felt expectant. It might have been waiting for us to do something, or waiting to pounce *if* we did something.

Either way, it was disorienting. It was hard to judge the distance between buildings, and I found myself staying near to Vance out of fear that we would be separated.

We briefly glimpsed the deathwitch, but this time she wasn't alone. The looks we received from those gathered around her fire, probably to mourn the young prince they were preparing to lose, sent Vance and me away quickly.

At last, we found Marcel at one of the common hearths. I considered asking about her offer to take me to human lands, and when she might be willing to make that trip, but she spoke first.

"I've volunteered to go with Shane," she said.

"You— He— How did you even know?" I stammered. Laurence had said he would ask for volunteers, but that had been just minutes ago. When he said it, I hadn't really believed anyone would offer without coercion. How could she have come to such a decision so quickly?

"I've gone many places, seen many things," Marcel said. "The way I see it, this is just one more journey for me to take. My magic will not harm anyone, even if the vampires get control of it. I am young and healthy enough to meet Jeshickah's requirements, but Andrew and I have been try-ing unsuccessfully for over a decade to have a child, so I have reason to hope I cannot give Midnight that satisfaction." Her voice sounded calm, but I didn't believe her. *Couldn't* believe her. "I am not the only one who has offered, and I do not know who the king will choose, but I wanted to let you know ... if I go, Andrew will help you search for your parents. He will want to leave here, anyway. If King Laurence does not choose me, then we will both travel with you, if you want us."

"I ... thank you," I whispered. I could hardly under-stand the words I was hearing. "You ... you're talking about selling yourself to Midnight. How can you possibly think of *me* at this time?"

Marcel smiled briefly. "My magic brought me to you years ago, Kadee. I do believe I saved your life, and I will never apologize for that, but you are a woman now, not a child. You have your own soul to guide you. If your path takes you back to the beginning, I would be honored to walk beside you, in spirit if not in flesh. For now, please excuse me, but I have affairs I must see to."

Once she was gone, Vance wrapped his arms around me, and I turned my face to bury it in his shoulder. How I wanted to tell the Shantel, *Don't do it, don't make a deal! Stand up and fight!* But I couldn't tell them to sacrifice everything for principles and hope.

Another sleepless night, and then we were back in the royal receiving room. King Laurence and Prince Lucas were inside, but Shane was not. The older sakkri was there with them, shaking her head.

"He came to speak to us last night," the sakkri explained, "and my sister left with him. I do not believe he has run from us, but I do know she is hiding him from us. My sister . . . she does not approve of this decision."

"How do you feel?" I asked.

The sakkri drew a deep breath, and closed her eyes. "My time here is nearly over. My power has lessened, and the land does not speak to me as clearly as it once did. I have had no vision about these days. I think perhaps my sister has."

"Then you think she is right?" Laurence asked.

"No." The answer was swift and unequivocal, and obviously took Laurence aback. "I think my sister has corrupted her power, and is listening to her own heart, instead of listening to the heart of the forest."

"How do we find her?" I asked.

"I had hoped she would come to us," the older sakkri said, sighing. "I do not like the notion of tracking her down like a beast in the woods."

"She seems to leave us no choice," Lucas said, falling into his throne with a frustrated cry. When he looked up at the sakkri again, his gaze was like that of a small child begging for comfort. "Are you sure we are doing the right thing?" he asked her.

"Chaos before the fall," she whispered. The air around her had gone still, and silent. My tongue seemed to lock in my mouth as I listened. "Each great nation will give its flesh and blood to the beast. Every land will know betrayal and bereavement. A white queen will rise in desperation and brutality. The line is drawn. Players take their places. The battle cannot be won, but it will not be lost."

Both of the Shantel men leapt forward to catch the sakkri as she collapsed, her prophecy complete.

I remembered what Marcel had told me—that a sakkri's prophecy always came true. Now, having heard what the

Shantel considered a true prophecy, I felt I knew even less than before.

What did any of that *mean*?

I wanted to ask a thousand questions, most notably about the "white queen" that the sakkri had referenced in a less than positive manner. Before I could, though, the receiving room doors burst open, and the younger sakkri leapt in, running like a gazelle to her sister's side.

"Are you all right?" she asked, as if she had not been hiding in the woods with the prince who now hung in the doorway behind her, looking guilty and resigned. Without speaking, Laurence nodded to one of the guards, who ushered Shane inside and moved to stand behind him so he could not slip away again. Then we all turned our eyes back to the two sakkri.

"I am sorry," the older sakkri said to her sister, the whisper choked by tears. "I see now what you saw, but you do not understand. You *cannot*—"

"We cannot save ourselves by selling our own," the younger sakkri insisted, looking back at Shane with tear-filled eyes.

"Your affection for the prince is clouding your judgment," the other sakkri replied. "Your affair with him . . . it should never have happened, sister, and this is why."

"Shane?" Lucas hissed, staring at his brother in shock.

Shane looked away, and took a step back . . . then defiantly moved forward again and knelt by the sakkri's side.

He touched her arm, to many protests from his brother and father, and implored her, "You need to let me go."

"I can*not*," the younger sakkri spat, rising to her feet and pushing them all away. "Do you not understand me? We cannot save ourselves if we pollute our own royal blood with slave-trading. I cannot change my belief on this, and the forest knows what I believe. I will not bend and neither will it."

I felt my breath leave me in a rush, as the sakkri spoke words that had bubbled inside me for days now. Each time, I had forced them back down because I felt we had no other choice, but now the most powerful woman in this land was stating as fact what I had wanted to cry in hopeless frustration.

"Shane—" She took a deep breath. "I love you. You know this. I have loved you for years, since we were both children and you came to the temple to study, and I will love you always, but it is not for you that I protest what we are doing here."

"If I do not go to Midnight," Shane said, slowly and deliberately, "then we will all die in this forest. You *saw* what their magic can do. You—"

"I will not allow it," the sakkri said simply in reply.

"But can you *stop* it?" Lucas demanded.

We all looked up as, outside, the wind began to howl, ripping through the trees around us and making them raise a mournful sound. I shuddered. I trusted the sakkri not to hurt her own people, but I was glad not to be out in the woods at that moment.

"Sister, please, see reason," the older sakkri begged.

"As you did, when you brought the Obsidian children here despite my pleas?" the younger sakkri said.

"I saw the fire that would engulf this land if we did not satisfy the blood-drinkers demands," the older one replied. "So did you! We have no way to stop it unless—"

Her sister interrupted her with five flat words: "*I* will go to Midnight."

"Absolutely not!" Laurence protested at the same moment that Shane said, "That *I* will not allow."

"Sister," the older sakkri said, grasping the other woman's hand. "My time here is nearly done. I will take my last breath before autumn ends. If you leave us, there will be no one to guide the next sakkri . . . if she will even be born, with your essence taken to foreign soil."

"Would you rather we all die here?" the younger sakkri asked.

"The land itself will not allow us to lose you!" the older sakkri cried. "The royal family is like the leaves of this forest. They come, and they fall in winter, and the land mourns them for a season until they are reborn. But we are the roots of this land. We cannot simply leave it. The land itself would hold you, even if we were all mad enough to give permission."

"We are not gods," the younger retorted, "and the roots

of a tree are no more immortal than its leaves. Entire trees may split and become rotten and hollow, a place for new life to begin in the place left behind."

I looked to Vance, wondering if he was as lost within all the nature analogies as I was.

"Is this argument getting us anywhere?" I interrupted. "Trees and roots and leaves are fine, and I know someone is going to tell me that occasionally an entire forest burns to the ground and the ash nurtures the soil, but I do not think any of us want to go that far."

Vance said, "Whether it is Shane or the sakkri, we need to—"

He broke off as the younger sakkri spun to stare at him, her eyes widening. "You're right," she said—but it did not sound like she was agreeing with his words. "There is only one way to end this."

Vance stepped back warily and said, "I am not sure I want to be—"

Graceful as a willow, or wind in the trees, the sakkri turned around. Her hand found the sword sheathed in the nearest guard's belt, and as she continued to turn, she raised that sword and turned it on Prince Lucas.

"What are you *doing*?" Shane yelped, jumping in the way as his brother narrowly dodged the blade. If he thought his lover would hesitate to hurt him, however, he was wrong. A red slash appeared across his chest.

I was standing near enough that Shane's blood splashed

me, hot on my skin. The very air around me quivered, as if it were in shock. What was she *doing*? Would she kill Shane to keep him from Midnight's grasp?

I heard shouting as guards scrambled to respond, but they were too slow. Royal Shantel blood flew across the reception hall as the blade made another arc, this time striking Shane in the arm he had raised to defend himself.

The blow was not fatal, but the shock and pain on Shane's face was stark, even before the sakkri shifted her grip and raised the sword a final time.

One of the guards put himself between Shane and the seemingly mad woman, but it was Lucas who changed shape and pounced. The older sakkri called his name, and the distance between his start and his target seemed to lengthen, so instead of cleanly driving her to the ground he managed only to rip claws in a line down her back.

She gasped, and stumbled to her knees. When she tried to stand, the guard who had tried to protect Shane grabbed her wrist, and took the sword from her grip. Lucas returned to human form and stared, horrified, at the sakkri's blood that remained on his hands.

Blood pooling on the ground beneath her, the younger sakkri looked up at Prince Lucas and said, "I have spilled the blood of the royal family. I have committed treason. The law says I must be executed. As your sakkri, I will offer one alternative: send me to Midnight. Otherwise you will be forced to kill me."

Wide-eyed, Lucas stammered, "We— I—" He looked to his father, whose face held the same horror, but with dawning resignation.

"The quetzal was bluffing when he threatened Shane," the sakkri snapped. Outside, the wind rose even louder. The building around us groaned under the force. "I am not. Let me go."

She stood, stumbled, and would have fallen if the guards had not caught her.

Laurence nodded. Lucas shut his eyes as he said, "Vance ... Kadee ... take her. Tell ... tell Midnight we have nothing of greater value to give."

CHAPTER 23

THE SAKKRI HOOKED an arm over Vance's shoulder so he could help her stand, and we limped out of the Family's receiving room.

We were still in the front hall when the fleshwitch who had treated me years ago approached us at a run, reeled upon seeing the sakkri, and started speaking rapidly to her in the Shantel's native language. The sakkri shook her head. When she replied, I only understood one word, but that was enough: "Shane." She was sending the healer to the prince.

Her lover, who she had assaulted—even threatened to kill—so she could take his place at Midnight.

"Can you heal yourself?" I asked as the fleshwitch disappeared inside and the sakkri let out another gasp of pain and seemed to collapse in Vance's arms. The ragged claw marks ran from her shoulder blades to the top of her hips, and were still bleeding freely.

She started to shake her head, and let out another little gasp instead.

Looking around desperately, I grabbed the first thing nearby—a wool tapestry depicting some kind of forest scene, which had been hanging on the wall. I didn't care what it showed. The scene turned red as I folded it and pressed it tightly against her skin. Vance added his hands to mine on the sakkri's prone body.

"She isn't going to be able to walk," he said.

"If one of you can help me, I can ride," the sakkri assured us, each word clipped with pain. "Tie off the bandage. We must go."

"Are you sure?"

As I tore strips of fabric from a table covering to better bandage the sakkri, I realized that none of the Shantel were in the room. Were they all preoccupied with Shane, or were they intentionally rejecting the sakkri?

"Will you be able to fight the vampires?" I asked as the sakkri once more struggled to stand. She was the most powerful magic user in this land, and she had taken Shane's place voluntarily—by force, even. She must have a plan.

"The sakkri is forbidden to shed blood, forbidden to be possessed," she replied. With short, painful strides, she led us to the stables. She leaned against the wall as Vance saddled two horses, who shied from the smell of blood. He murmured soothingly to them as the sakkri continued to speak. "I can already feel the land rejecting me for what I have done here. Once I cross Midnight's threshold and declare myself their property, the bond will be severed."

The sakkri rode in front of Vance, his arms around her obviously the only thing keeping her in the saddle.

We reached the edge of Shantel land sooner than all logic said we could. This land wanted us gone, *quickly*. The sakkri had healed enough to walk, slowly, so we released the horses before we left the Shantel forest. The sakkri assured us they would find their way home. Her wounds had started to knit shut, enough that the heavy bandages were no longer necessary.

I was not comforted by how fast she healed. Midnight would surely make use of it.

We reached Midnight midmorning the next day. I never would have had the nerve, but as soon as the guards had let us by, Vance knocked loudly on one of the trainer's doors. It seemed to take forever for Jaguar to answer, half dressed, hair mussed as if he had been roused from sleep.

His expression snapped from irritation to surprise and then amusement within moments.

"Is this from you two, or from the Shantel?" he asked, regarding the sakkri with a thoughtful gaze.

"From the Shantel," Vance answered. "She is . . . was . . . their sakkri. You won't get anything more from them."

"I suspect not," Jaguar replied. "Very well. I will speak

to Jeshickah, but I believe she will agree this is acceptable. Come here, pet," he ordered the witch, who balked at the endearment . . . and then stepped forward, acknowledging the name as her own with a shudder.

I turned away as a chill ran up my back, though I couldn't help but hear Jaguar's parting words.

"You both stink of blood, and it's not all hers."

Vance shut the door, sparing us the need to reply.

We didn't even consider staying to bathe in Midnight, though I had seen their luxurious washrooms. Instead, the first time we crossed a stream, Vance and I both stripped down one at a time and kept watch for each other so we could wash our bodies and clothes as thoroughly as possible in the icy water. Shivering, we paused long enough to dry our gear by a fire, and then we moved on.

"How dangerous is it for the sakkri to be in Midnight's hands?" Vance asked me as we walked toward serpiente land, and the Obsidian guild's main camp. We had spoken before of going back to the Shantel, about seeking my parents with Marcel's or Andrew's help, but after that bloodbath, I didn't dare go back so soon. "They have been trying to acquire magic users for years now."

"She isn't the sakkri anymore," I answered, remembering what she had said about the land rejecting her. "Once she allows herself to be owned, she will lose her connection to her power. At least, that is what the Shantel believe."

"Maybe she has an elaborate plan to kill them all,"

Vance suggested. "Maybe she sold herself so she could get close enough."

"I don't know." How much power did the sakkri have outside of Shantel land? Most of what I knew of Shantel power boiled down to illusions, but a deathwitch exiled for years from Shantel land had still been strong enough to turn Vance into a deadly weapon. Who knew what a sakkri could do? "I wish we knew," I added.

We hadn't started any of this, but we had been bloodied by it. We had been forced to witness.

We both slept restlessly that night, and the five that followed as we returned with heavy steps to the main Obsidian camp. Sometimes my nightmares featured a fire that burned with magic, devouring everything in its path. Sometimes I saw the sakkri, or Alasdair, or Misha, or Shkei, and they were screaming.

Never again.

Vance and I did not speak more about leaving; I did not dare return to Shantel land to find Marcel, and I did not have the heart for a new adventure.

I would decide what to do about *King* Aaron if he actually took the throne. I would respond to *Queen* Misha if Aaron took her as his mate and the serpiente people didn't murder her in her bed. I would stand with them against Midnight if the time came, and we had anywhere to stand. Until then, I would hold my own counsel about prophecies and fate.

We were between the serpiente palace and the main Obsidian camp when a thrashing nearby in the woods caused us both to reach for weapons. With my thoughts so dark and my nerves so tight, I nearly put an arrow in Aaron before he raised his hands and hissed, "Kadee, it's me! Please, help."

He was dressed in nothing but light pants that were better designed for dancing than hiking; they had been torn in multiple places by the forest, and he had a scrape on his arm as if he had fallen at least once. There were tears on his face, and as far as I could tell, no guard in his wake.

I continued to scan the forest behind him and around us as I said quietly, "You're hurt. What happened?"

"He told me to leave," Aaron whispered. "I came to warn them, as soon as I heard I ran to the camp to warn them, but then the guards were there and you have to believe me I wanted to fight but Farrell told me to leave. That I couldn't afford for the guards to see me with them. Hara sent them because she saw Misha with me and knew the guild had to be close. Farrell said that if they were Hara's guards, they would probably kill me and tell Julian the guild was responsible."

Two words of the breathy ramble made it into my mind: *Farrell* and *guards*.

Farrell had told his son to run. Of course he had.

I said the same thing. "You get back to the palace. You're not a fighter. We will send someone to you when it is safe."

What I did not add was *You probably led the guards right*

to us, you fool! They would never have found our camp on their own.

Then Vance and I were sprinting through the forest, praying we reached the camp in time. They would have fled if they had been able.

Please, God, please let them be safe, I prayed as I ran.

My own hypocrisy was stifling. How many minutes before had I been wishing I did not need to face any of them?

I don't want them dead.

I tripped over one fallen soldier, at the edge of what had been our camp. I took his weapon, a short-sword I could swing in close quarters where my bow was impractical, and then we continued to track the fight. Our guild was obviously trying to retreat, but the other serpiente were pursuing instead of giving up the chase the way they normally did. How many soldiers had Hara *sent*—the entire palace guard?

Against a clan accused of murdering one royal and abducting another? I thought. *Why would she send anything less than a lethal force?*

Vance and I had each taken out one of the soldiers furthest back before our presence was noted, and then we had to fade into the forest. Neither of us had the skills to engage in a fair fight with a trained soldier. I had rarely wished more fervently that Vance really had a bloodwitch's magic.

We circled around in time to see most of our kin with their backs to the spring-swollen Salmon River. This was where many forest travelers lost their lives if they were not careful and did not know where the bridges and safe spaces to ford were.

This was not one of those places.

I suddenly remembered my dream about the river ... but there was no bridge here. Vance and I arrived just in time to see Farrell put himself between two guards and Misha. He shouted to her, "Go!" and it became clear that the other members of our guild were mostly fighting because she still was.

Farrell threw a dagger at a third soldier, who had been a hairsbreadth from knocking Aika into the river. It sank into his thigh.

The moment of distraction probably saved Aika's life, but it was costly. Another soldier got inside Farrell's guard. I saw Farrell's eyes widen with surprise as a sword pierced his side, puncturing the abdomen, unhindered by any bones. Such a fragile spot. I drew my bow, whispered a prayer to any god who might be listening, and let fly. The arrow struck the guard's shoulder, nestling into the armor with enough force to at least make him recoil and look up for the threat, pulling his sword free.

As Aika and Torquil kicked the soldier who had engaged them into the river, I nocked another arrow. Misha slammed a stave into the back of the skull of the one I had hit, so I turned my bow on another who had been creeping up on Malachi with a dagger in his hand. This time my aim was true, and the arrowhead pierced the unprotected flesh at the guard's throat.

Malachi, who was bloodied and unarmed, turned with surprise as the guard behind him fell. Then, as I watched, he pounced and dragged another soldier into the river. Both figures disappeared beneath the rolling water.

At last, the woods were silent. Seven soldiers were dead, two lost in the river, and the other five in the woods between the original camp and the final battle. What of our people?

I ran and fell to my knees next to Farrell, reaching him just as Aika let out a wail of despair that told me everything I feared. Torquil was desperately holding a bandage to the wound in Farrell's side, but even I could tell it was too late.

CHAPTER 24

FARRELL'S GRAY EYES were open, but they stared at another world. No breath moved his chest.

Others gathered near, creeping close and whispering things like "He's all right, isn't he?" I felt Vance's warmth at my side as he came close and wrapped an arm around me, but I couldn't look away from Farrell's pale face and quickly misting gray eyes. Someone else took the bow from my clenched hands. If only I had been a little faster . . . if my aim had been a little truer . . .

How could such an important man die so swiftly, with no warning? No final, dramatic words of wisdom, or caution, or love. Just gone, senselessly. He had sent Aaron away and then protected Misha. Always Misha.

"Aaron led them to us," Aika said, her voice low and

trembling. "We all could have run if he had not brought the soldiers inside the camp."

"He was trying to warn us," Torquil replied hotly. "We cannot blame him for being a fool."

"*Hara* sent them," Misha spat. "That is what matters. Aaron did not intend to betray us. Hara is the one who called for our deaths."

I reached out to close Farrell's eyes, but my hand froze above his brow, unable to complete its task. How could I hide the eyes that had seen a future in this world no one else could even imagine, where freedom was possible?

"Where is Malachi?" Vance asked. "I thought I saw him go into the river."

My heart constricted even more, but Misha just shook her head. "I can sense him downriver. He is cold and wet but will return to us soon."

Misha's hand knocked mine aside and smoothed Farrell's eyelids down, shutting those gray eyes away forever.

"Do we build a pyre?" Vance asked, obviously less concerned with blame and vengeance than with the proper treatment of the deceased.

"Yes," I answered.

By the time Malachi came limping back into camp, sodden and bruised—and certainly the only one of us hardy enough to navigate the river currents and return alive—we were struggling to gather enough supplies to create the pyre. The wood was soaked from recent rain, and there was little good kindling to be found.

"Your magic is dormant," Malachi said to Vance, "but I think I can use it to focus mine, to make the fire burn hotter and longer. We will send him off properly."

Vance nodded, looking dazed, and simply extended an arm toward Malachi. Blood was the source of his power. He neither questioned nor objected when Malachi took a blade to his flesh. I remembered Stefan saying, *Let me use his blood, and I can make you a spark that will burn stone.*

I looked away, which meant my gaze was on Misha when she began to speak.

"I am tired," she said softly, "of losing our own kin because of Cobriana *spite*. I went to the palace without pretense," she said, her gaze falling to one of the soldiers' bodies, "but my very presence there was apparently enough of a threat to Cobriana pride that Hara felt it was appropriate to send a *death squad* against us. Some of us were innocent before, but anyone who defended himself or herself today is now guilty of treason for raising a hand against royal guards, as these were."

She paused to take a breath. Malachi and Vance succeeded in making the fire catch, and suddenly flames were rising into the night.

Aaron crept back into camp beside me. His face was white as he beheld the rising flames, and asked, "Who did we lose?"

For a moment, there was no sound but the crackling whisper of the pyre. It took me two tries to say "Farrell."

He swayed, and let out a wail so heartfelt it made me shudder. He stumbled toward the fire until he was close enough that others pushed him back before he could burn himself. Misha went to his side, and grasped his hand.

"I see only one real, appropriate response," Misha said as we all moved to surround the flames, drawing in their warmth and trying to find some form of strength, or comfort.

I am sorry, I thought to Farrell. *I wish I had had a chance to speak to you again before now.*

I was barely listening to Misha as she explained, "While I was in Midnight, I spoke to one of their trainers. I propose that, before the Cobriana princess can send any more of us to our graves or worse, we send her to the fate she would declare for all of us if she has the chance."

I must have misheard her.

Torquil replied, "Hear, hear," as if Misha's suggestion was indeed appropriate, and I heard murmurs of agreement from the others.

"Excuse me?" I asked.

"I made a deal," Misha clarified. "If we can get Hara out of the palace without a fuss, Midnight will quietly take her off our hands. With her gone, Aaron is heir. When he takes the throne—"

"You're *mad*," I interrupted. "I have no love for Hara,

but you cannot possibly think it is acceptable to sell someone into that place just to get her out of your way!"

The voices of the trainers paraded through my head.
Jaguar murmuring, *Come here, pet,* to the woman who had so
recently been the most revered woman among the Shantel.
Gabriel asking, *Did you ever meet my Ashley?* Jeshickah telling Vance she would accept lesser payment from the Shantel, *if you were willing to work to make up the difference.*

I always have time to make deals with your guild, Gabriel
had said. *You do offer the prettiest toys.*

Misha must have made her deal with him just moments
before. No wonder Jeshickah had made a point to clarify
that Vance's agreement with the Shantel would apply to
future negotiations, so it wouldn't ... how had Jeshickah
put it? *Complicate other business.*

"Just for that?" Aaron echoed. His gaze was on the
pyre, hot before us. "No, not *just* for that."

"Absolutely not," Malachi said, speaking up. My heart
lightened. People were angry and hurt and wanted to lash
out, but they would listen to Malachi. "The *last* thing Farrell would have wanted is for us to engage in the slave trade
to—"

"*The last thing Farrell wanted,*" Aaron spat, "was my
safety. He shoved me away. He told me to run. He told me
that I *needed* to take the throne, that I could not be caught
in this fight. He died for that idea."

Vance's voice was harsh as he told Misha, "If you do

this, you'll be no better than Hara. She sold your brother and you. Now you want to even the scales by wallowing in the same sin?"

"*Sin?*" Misha echoed. "If you're offended by what we do here, go back to your masters. I'll send you with Hara if you like."

Malachi gasped. "I will not allow—"

"*Allow?*" Misha snapped. "We are the Obsidian guild, Malachi, and Aaron is a prince. We bow to no master, least of all you. You allow us nothing. If you are not with us, you can get out of this camp."

My voice seemed to escape me before my mind caught up, and I heard myself say, "I am with Malachi. I am sick of this, trading and selling and buying flesh. It's disgusting, and degrading, and it will destroy us all. Farrell would never—"

Misha's slap caught me by surprise. My head whipped to the side and my ears rang as she said, "If you refuse to stand with me, and to obey Farrell's dying wishes, then you have no right to speak his name."

"Misha, think about what you're doing," Malachi pleaded, an instant before Vance caught Misha by the arm and dragged her away from me, shouting, "Keep your hands to yourself, or—"

Fighting.

My own kin were suddenly at each other's throats. I couldn't understand it. I didn't *want* to understand it. Far-

274

rell was dead, and now the only family I had left was tearing itself apart. Torquil had leapt to Misha's defense, and swung a punch at Vance, while Aika finally let loose months of simmering anger and grabbed Misha by the throat.

Malachi stepped between Vance and Torquil while I tried to plead with Aika to release Misha. Not long ago, we had unleashed this violence against guards who had been sent to kill us, and left their bodies in the woods for the scavengers. No matter how we disagreed, I did not want to see the same deadly force unleashed against our own people.

I saw Torquil throw Malachi to the ground at the same time that Misha got a knee up and kicked Aika away. She shouted at me, "This is the only way! How can you not see that?"

"Everyone, you need to calm down," Aaron pleaded. He knelt next to Malachi, holding up a hand to try to keep Torquil back as he pleaded, "Malachi, we need you with us. You have been our guiding light, our prophet, since before I was born. We—"

"Stop saying *we*," Malachi snapped, shoving the prince of the serpiente away so he sprawled in the dirt. "You are not *us*. You are not Obsidian. You are—"

"I am Farrell Obsidian's son!" Aaron protested.

"And Farrell is *dead*!" Malachi shouted.

The words seemed to echo long in the woods. *Farrell is dead.*

Voices overlapped, protesting, shouting, crying, chaos,

but Torquil's cut through the rest to say almost calmly, "Does anyone else hear that?"

When our shouting ceased, the sound of hurrying footsteps in the woods was clear. More guards.

"Aaron, can you help us?" Torquil asked.

Aaron replied, "I need to go. Misha—"

"Coward," Vance spat. "You say you're one of us, but you'll run as soon as—"

"Stop it!" I hissed. If there were guards coming our way, we couldn't afford to stand here bickering. "We need to go. Malachi—"

Aaron disappeared into the shadows before the guards broke into the clearing. Most of the others fled, but Malachi seemed to freeze, staring at the space where his sister had been.

"Malachi," I repeated as I reached for my dagger. I wouldn't leave him alone.

"Kadee . . ." Vance had stayed with me, and drawn his own weapon, but his body was trembling with exhaustion and fear as he moved to set his shoulder next to mine.

On Malachi's other side, I glimpsed Aika with her stave in her hands.

The guards who had us in their sights seemed to be waiting. Were they nervous to approach the Obsidian guild's famous half-falcon witch . . . or did they just know they had even more backup on the way?

Malachi took a deep breath, and I saw his eyes flicker around us.

"We run," he said. The words were soft, but the power of them flowed over me, through me. I dropped the weapon in my hand, saving the instant it would have taken to sheathe it. Aika and Vance did so with equal hesitation, and like a flock of birds that shifts direction without warning, we fled together.

For the last score of years, the legend had built that the Obsidian guild was capable of disappearing without a trace. I could feel Malachi's magic struggling to hide us now, but there was a difference between hiding in plain sight and disappearing once seen.

We ran, and the guards chased, and the night became darker.

Where were the others?

Do not think of them now, I commanded myself. *Protect yourself, and those who stand with you.*

I let out a yelp of surprise when Malachi grabbed my hand and yanked me down, drawing Vance with us at the same time. Aika followed without questioning, and then I realized we were in a grove of white birch trees. I could see Malachi's lips moving as if in prayer, but I could not hear the words he whispered.

Three of the guards who had been chasing us came as close as the edge of our birch refuge, but Malachi's magic kept them from noticing us there. I thought the rapid patter of Vance's heart might deafen me as he leaned against me, and I held him tightly. I felt the madness rise in him, the fear of captivity that made him want to launch himself at the white bars of our self-imposed cage and draw blood from our captors, who shook their heads and began to make camp only a few yards away from our refuge.

Why were there just four of us here? Were we really the only ones who had stood with Malachi instead of following Misha?

I realized Malachi was looking at me. Softly, he said, "The spell a white viper spins is like a spiderweb. It is nearly invisible, even to one caught in its trap." I looked nervously to the guards, so near our hiding space, but they did not seem to hear Malachi's hushed voice. "You two were away and Aika always avoided her, but Misha has snared Aaron so tightly that he has no choice but to follow her and the others . . . even Torquil. . . ." He looked at Aika, whose mate had gone the other way when our group had split. "I think Farrell might have been able to stand up to her still, if—"

His breath hitched. As if the sound had given me permission, I felt the first sob break its way out of my chest.

⌇

I'm not sure if I slept, or simply passed the night in an exhausted, numb fugue. Sometime in the rainy morning I found myself asking Malachi, "Do we have . . . any kind of plan?"

"I don't know," our prophet said. He looked toward

where the serpiente guards had been, but they had moved on as soon as dawn turned the black skies gray.

"We need to warn Hara," Vance said. His expression twisted as if he had tasted something sour before he added, "Carefully. I don't imagine she will welcome us gratefully if we go speak to her, even if we are trying to protect her."

Hara was a symptom, not the problem. "We need to stop Misha," I said.

"Do we?" Aika asked. "I don't approve of her methods, but she is the one who is supposed to—"

"I'm sick of *prophecy*," I snapped. I met Malachi's pale gaze without flinching. "I'm sorry, but I am. I'm sick of us following what some vision says. We sold Alasdair to Midnight. We helped the Shantel sell the sakkri to Midnight, too. Now Misha and Aaron are working to sell Hara Kiesha Cobriana to Midnight. If we continue this way, pretty soon every royal house of the shapeshifters will be owned by the vampires."

The sakkri's prophecy echoed in my mind: *Each great nation will give its flesh and blood to the beast. Every land will know betrayal and bereavement. A white queen will rise in desperation and brutality. The line is drawn. Players take their places. The battle cannot be won, but it will not be lost.*

It was time to draw the line. It was time to admit that sometimes, mere survival wasn't enough.

It was time to make a stand.

ABOUT THE AUTHOR

AMELIA ATWATER-RHODES wrote her first novel, *In the Forests of the Night*, when she was thirteen. Other books in the Den of Shadows series are *Demon in My View*, *Shattered Mirror*, *Midnight Predator*, *Persistence of Memory*, *Token of Darkness*, *All Just Glass*, *Poison Tree*, and *Promises to Keep*. She has also published the five-volume series The Kiesha'ra: *Hawksong*, a *School Library Journal* Best Book of the Year and a *Voice of Youth Advocates* Best Science Fiction, Fantasy, and Horror Selection; *Snakecharm*; *Falcondance*; *Wolfcry*, an IRA-CBC Young Adults' Choice; and *Wyvernhail*. Her most recent novel is *Bloodwitch* (The Maeve'ra: Volume One). Visit her online at AmeliaAtwaterRhodes.com.